OTHER BOOKS
BY HAROLD JAFFE

EROS
ANTI-EROS

HAROLD JAFFE

CITY LIGHTS BOOKS
San Francisco

First published by City Lights Books in 1990

Cover design: John Miller / Black and White Design
Cover Photograph: Kathryn Macdonald
Votive courtesy: Joan Walsh
Book design: Patricia Fuji

LIBRARY OF CONGRESS CATALOGING-IN-PUBLICATION DATA

Jaffe, Harold.
  Eros, Anti-Eros. / Harold Jaffe
    p.   cm.
  ISBN 0-87286-245-3 $21.95 ISBN 0-87286-246-1 (pbk.) $6.95
  I. Title
  PS3560.A312E76 1990
  813'.54--dc20 89-7795
  CIP

City Lights Books are available to bookstores through our primary
distributor: Subterranean Company, P.O. Box 168, 265 S. 5th
Street, Monroe, Oregon 97456. (503) 847-5274. Our books are
also available through library jobbers and regional distributors. For
personal orders and catalogs, please write to City Lights Books, 261
Columbus Avenue, San Francisco, CA 94133.

CITY LIGHTS BOOKS are edited by Lawrence Ferlinghetti and
Nancy J. Peters and published at the City Lights Bookstore, 261
Columbus Avenue, San Francisco, Ca 94133.

ACKNOWLEDGEMENTS

Several of the texts from *Eros: Anti-Eros* were published in journals, specifically: "Eros / Calvin Klein" and "Eros / Xerox" in *City Lights Review*; "Eros / Duras" and "Eros / Skinhead" in *Central Park*; "Eros / Exxon" in *Witness*; "Eros / Talk Dirty" in *Black Ice*; "Eros / Assault Rifle" in *Mississippi Review*; and an abstract of various other texts in *Cream City Review*.

I'd like to thank Jim Scully, Ken Jones, Harry Polkinhorn, Larry McCaffery, Michael Krekorian, and Maggie Jaffe for reading and commenting on this text in manuscript.

CONTENTS

ONE

TWO

This book is for people living with AIDS

ONE

The continued repressive organization of the instincts seems to be necessitated less by the "struggle for existence" than by the interest in prolonging this struggle—by the interest in domination.

Herbert Marcuse
Eros and Civilization

Everyone detected with AIDS should be tattooed in the upper forearm, to protect common-needle users, and on the buttocks, to prevent the victimization of other homosexuals.

William F. Buckley

EROS /
Calvin Klein

This is the price of seduction.
The secret must not be
broken, at the risk of the
story's falling into banality.

Jean Beaudrillard

He was sipping coffee from a fur coffee cup thinking of the bombing of Nicaragua when she drifted over, sat down, set her elbows on the table, stared at him bemusedly, said matter of factly:

"You're drinking chemistry not coffee, which if injected intramuscularly would numb your extremities and make your eyes tear at the playing of our national anthem."

He set his fur coffee cup down on the French café-style tablecloth, in the museum members' "penthouse," high above the moiling city, far below the executive decisions to bomb Nicaragua, Nicaraguas.

"Do you come here often?"

He said he did, she said she wasn't surprised, still bent forward on her elbows, with her ironic appraising look. He decided to appraise *her,* leaning back, inferring her back from her front, sine-curve front.

"Can I buy you a coffee?"

She smiled. "Dry white wine."

"Miss, what kind of dry white do you have?"

"Chablis."

"Is it nice?"

"Nobody's complained that I know of."

"Two glasses please."

Still smiling: reassuringly unstraightened teeth, wide mouth, fleshy lower lip, a European mouth, French? Her clear dark eyes did not seem precisely French, seemed Turkish/Greek/Armenian, one of the lesser Euros, "Oriental" virtually, pigmented (virtually), requiring special dispensation to join the European Economic Community, a.k.a. the Common Market, presided over by uncommon communalists, with their in-common devotion to anti-communism . . .

"Shut your brain off," she said, "sit next to me."

He moved his chair close to hers, panning the café, about two/thirds filled.

The wine came.

"Here's to old friends."

It wasn't cold, so-so dry.

"What do you mean *old* friends?" he said.

"I feel like I know you," she said. "Hyperactive brain, outsize heart, Calvin Klein briefs, big but not big-big dick . . ."

And suddenly they were prone, no, side-by-side, well, her back to his side, long lovely back, his tongue to her vertebrae, sweet-smelling bone-pearls, one of her slim arms extended behind her, rubbing-stroking his, what did she mean not big-big, sure big was nice, but big-big was nicer, obviously he was big, he knew that, but wasn't he at least fractionally big-big, wouldn't she grant him that? No she wouldn't, not in this ungenerous time/juncture/gash, no more Ms. nice gal . . .

"Stop squirming."

"I was thinking."

"If this," she said, "were *Before AIDS*, we'd be out of here, your flat, mine, you'd be sipping, not squirming, real wine out of platonic slippers, I have graceful feet, slender as rain, preliminary to guess what?"

"The beast with two backs?"

"Sounds familiar. I guess that means fucking. Old Testament?"

"Shakespeare. Now *you're* squirming."

"Good thing I wore a skirt."

"Nice long legs, I like your scent. Poison?"

"No, that's the well-bred woman to our right."

For they were still in the museum members' penthouse café, sitting very close to each other, high above the hunger armies, underwritten by a grant from Mobil, far below the executive caveats on AIDS, the worst plague to plague the First World since the African blacks inflicted their slavery on these amber waves of Lite Beer and provoked a Civil War, *you versus yawl.*

"Raise your haunch, but *doucement.* Do you want to talk dirty?"

"How would you know I wasn't big-big?"

"You *are* a worrier. I said you were big, how much of the sweet life do you need? How would I know? I can tell, intuition, women have it, the heft of your thigh, and animals, I've seen you before, in this museum, gazing at your reflection as you gazed at paintings, in their glass frames, I've watched you walk, with your hands in your pockets, groping yourself while you looked at yourself looking at Grosz or Rouault, Giacometti, through your Calvin Klein briefs, thinking, dreamthinking, that's how I know."

And suddenly they were nude, check that, *naked,* sitting on the East Indian rug facing each other, at five paces, then drawing closer, sliding their hot haunches along the rug, she mounting him, settling on to his big, but not big-big, in Shiva-Shakti, yab-yum, her tongue in his mouth, no, check that, AIDS can be passed via saliva, certainly via bleeding gums, and periodontal maladies are among the signature ailments of our time, along with stress and jock-itch and real-estating wilderness and ass-licking (I'm speaking metaphorically).

"Can I get you folks more Chablis?"

"Like another?"

"I would."

"Two more please."

"That was close," he said.

"Close is exhilarating," she said. "Twist your hip."

"Soft skin," he said, "and slender, I can tell, as rain, do you do this a lot?"

Gentrified tinkle of fork/knife/china, the woman in Poison eating her tart with fork concave side down, in the European manner, obliquely facing them, her tablemate with hennaed hair to combat the gray, in gray blazer, corporate crest on hanky pocket, sipping his white.

Smile. "I try to do it where there's cause. Museum-corp-penthouse, Warhols on the walls, AIDS, Poison by Dior, a fetching other, yourself. I've watched you, an *interesting* neurotic, respects women, anatomizes them, it's a privilege to assault your brain/briefs, two scoops for the price of one, exotically flavored, family- but *not* jumbo-size, tattooed with wandering, because you've been places, I know you have. Now comes the hard part, I'm wasp-waisted."

"I believe it."

"Don't look down."

"Well, the decal on my left thigh reads Adolph, on my right, Coors. I have Manville on my chest, the good-hands folks who brought you asbestosis. On my big but not big-big: the boycotted grapes of Gallo, rich red wine, you can cut it with a knife. Futures brokers' salaries run up and down my spine, like sutures, like the Frankenstein monsters of the old black and white flicks, recently *colorized*, a fine example, if you need one, of state-of-the-art technology addressing itself to art and entertainment. I've been places, like you said."

"Can I slip in a word or two about myself?"

"Only if it relates to me."

"I come from a long line of vermin."

"My foot is stuck, hold still a minute."

"Ruling-class WASPS."

"Very delicate, nylon?"

"Spandex, stretchy. While the males enter the lists, the females oil their loins. While the males phone-order boxer shorts by the half-dozen from Banana Republic, the females take small risks, like graduated doses of arsenic. While the crested count, the cleft calculate, which is how I stumbled across your bad self, slim and soulful, dicey."

6

"But what if I were plump and soulful, like Orson Welles, say, or Diego Rivera, or Brando after *Last Tango*?"

"Here you are, two more Chablis, would you like to try a plum tart, freshly baked?"

"Baked where, not in the museum?"

"No, in the Bronx."

"I don't think so, thanks."

She: "Courtesy to the underclass."

He: "I'm closer to under than over."

She: "I think she saw you squirm."

He: "The tablecloth helps."

She: "I've done it without."

He: "Your dress is an advantage."

She: "My impression of you is you're stuck."

"Hmm. Yesterday while swimming laps in an indoor pool, too warm, thickly chlorinated, I imagined I was closely watching another *Kristallnacht:* Boer-like police in contaminant-resistant riot-gear brutally mustering AIDS victims. I was close to the situation physically, but not clearly situated, somehow, and evidently not visible, because I was witnessing while writing, typing on a small typewriter in my lap."

"Another *Kristallnacht?*"

"Yes."

"Typewriter on your lap?"

"Yes."

"Were you groping yourself while you witnessed?"

"I don't think so."

"What are you doing now?"

"Where?"

"Under the table?"

"Zippering up my pants. Your panties feel like the bandage on my appendicitis incision when I was a child. Only sexier. And fragrant. Spandex?"

"Uh-huh."

"Color?"

"Jade."

"Ah. Another Chablis?" he offered.

"No more Chablis," she said.

"You all gussied up?"

7

"I'm real comfy in your Calvin Klein's. Bit roomier than I'm used to. Waist size 34?"

"Uncanny."

"Sky blue?"

"Lapis."

"Very nice."

"Shall we?"

"Yes."

He pays the check, factors in the tip, they walk through the two-thirds-filled museum penthouse café to the elevator, press M for Main. An aerial view will show them filing through the exit area into the street, then forking: he west through the gauntlet of camped-out homeless, toward gusty Avenue of the Americas, she east, toward gusty Madison Avenue, he walking constrainedly in her wasp-waisted jade spandex, she gliding lithely in his lapis Calvin Kleins.

EROS /
Medical Waste

RAPTURE

Do you remember the young French actor who played the pining, passionate devotee of the beautiful black mezzo in *Diva?*

That's how Jean-Marc looks: slender, seventeen years old, with long-lashed dark eyes and a mercurial grace (see how he tosses his head).

Jean-Marc was visiting New York City with his mother Beatrice and her twin sister Josette. His father Marcel remained in Bordeaux where he was fastened to his work (this is a recent affliction among the bourgeois French, contracted from their contemptible Uncle Sam, along with "winning ugly," AIDS, barbecued burgers, and anti-abortion hysteria).

Today Jean-Marc was alone while Beatrice/Josette did Madison Avenue, window shopping, stopping in the Whitney Museum of American Art on 74th Street for a coffee, since though they are bourgeois they are not philistine. Moreover they think of American art, when they think of it at all, as a kind of folk art, equivalent more or less to going to the movies.

Which brings us back to *Diva* and Jean-Marc solo in the Big Apple, getting out of the subway at Times Square, walking west to 8th Avenue, then north, turning east at 57th Street and finding his way to Central Park South, home to expensive dentistry and the Plaza Cinema, which this fortnight is featuring *La Balance*, a "brutal, hard-boiled, American-style" French police drama.

Jean-Marc had no intention of going to the movies on a sunny October day in New York City, especially as day after tomorrow he would be returning to France. He consulted his small map and was about to turn north, when his eyes met the eyes of a girl who had just come out of the cinema.

And what eyes they were: large, long-lashed, wide-apart, blue as the sky in a Matisse canvas from his Nice period (don't be surprised at this reference: "high" culture is still institutionalized in Gaul).

She smiled, came right up to him.

"Are you lost?"

He shrugged. "I thought to walk in Central Park."

"Well, I'm walking up to 96th Street." (In truth she was going beyond 96th, into Spanish Harlem.) "We can walk together. Would you like that?"

"Yez, I would like eet."

"Are you German?"

"French."

"What a coincidence. I just saw this French movie, *La Balance*."

They were walking north.

"My name is Sandi. What's yours?"

"Jean-Marc."

They shook hands, her hand was larger than his.

"Jean-Marc. Nice name. The reason why I thought you maybe were German is we get a lot of German tourists in

10

New York. Japanese too, but I could tell you weren't Japanese."

Both laughed.

They sidestepped a knot of homeless who had left their benches alongside the park to panhandle. One of them badgered Jean-Marc and Sandi for several blocks.

"You from Paris?"

"Bordeaux."

"Bordeaux? Like the wine, right?"

He smiled. "Yes."

"I like wine a lot, but mostly I drink white. I like this one white in particular. Bal . . . Balance? No, that's the movie." She smiled. "I can't remember the name of the wine, but it's real good, not sweet. Fizzy, like champagne."

"Champagne?"

"Yes. I bet you like champagne. Am I right?"

Jean-Marc admitted liking champagne. They both smiled. They held hands.

An aerial shot will capture them: the slim, graceful French boy and the fractionally less graceful girl, somewhat taller than Jean-Marc, lithe in her movements, with big hands and big feet.

And now they are drawing close to royalty: the Metropolitan Museum of Art. Consider the "primitive" Rockefeller wing: entire villages in Africa / Mesoamerica / South America / the South Pacific stripped of their sacred-cultural infrastructures: temple facades, tree-tall totems, prows of boats, arches, tombs, shrines: not one or two of each but a dozen, twenty, side-by-side, like huge slabs of beef hooked and hanging in the freezers of a grand hotel, vast temperature-controlled gallery after gallery filled with booty.

North of the museum, on the grass, is a juggler in a Reagan clown costume: pointed head, orange hair, moronic smile. He is juggling six balls shaped like globes. One of the "globes" falls on the hard grass and explodes, like a cherry bomb. It's part of the act. The small crowd claps its approval. Sandi and Jean-Marc laugh and clap. They kiss. They kiss again, open-mouthed, lingering.

"Mmm, I liked that. Is that how they kiss in France?"

Jean-Marc shrugged, smiled.

"You are shy, aren't you?"

11

They were walking again.

"Shy?"

"Yes. You don't know what that word means? Sort of . . . well, it's hard to explain. But I like it. I like it in a man, or boy, whatever."

Jean-Marc didn't know what shy was exactly, but he knew what luck was and he was feeling lucky. She was beautiful and sexy and she liked him. She seemed to like him enough to have sex with him. But where? Maybe on the grass in the park, if they could find a private spot.

Sandi was an intuitive person and she liked Jean-Marc as soon as she saw him. She'd like to make love with him too. The problem was she couldn't, not in the way he'd expect, not yet.

Sandi, formerly Santos, was a pre-op transsexual, who had been receiving "hormone therapy" for sixteen months, and who was scheduled to have radical surgery the following Wednesday. Though she didn't look it, Sandi with her Matisse-blue eyes was born on the carefree, sun-kissed isle of Puerto Rico.

They passed the Guggenheim Museum which was running a *Futurismo* retrospective.

They passed the Mount Sinai Hospital complex, which bordered Spanish Harlem, where Sandi lived with her mother and two sisters. It was in Mount Sinai that Sandi would be operated on. The surgeon was Dr. Raoul Lewisohn, tall, wide-hipped, with a salt and pepper goatee, and the dominant figure in this sort of surgery on the East Coast. It was even rumored that Dr. Lewisohn was himself "post-op," but that is a vicious slander.

They passed other things, landmarks and stuff, but Sandi was concentrating on leading Jean-Marc to a spot in the park near 103rd Street where they could be alone, that is if the junkies left them alone. It was still early, a quarter to four, she didn't think the junkies would be a problem.

The spot, an entwined cluster of blackberry bushes, seemed to be unoccupied.

"Careful," she said, "of the needles. Junkies throw away their needles here."

She sat in the grass and he sat next to her. Soon they lay in each other's arms, kissing, stroking, pressing their bodies.

Sandi let Jean-Marc caress and kiss her small breasts, but that was it, nothing below the waist.

Jean-Marc was only a little disappointed, he assumed she had her period, anyway she stroked *him* below the waist, and sucked him too, and it felt wonderful.

Afterwards they walked, lightly/blithely, arms around each other's waist, in the direction of the setting sun and West End Avenue. They paused for espresso at a romantic little bistro on Columbus. Then they walked south to Lincoln Center, where the Metropolitan Opera was doing *Bôhème*, with the soulful soprano Teresa Stratas.

It was getting late but they couldn't part.

What did they talk about?

Love. And reuniting in France. Bordeaux. Going from there to Paris, renting a flat/garret/atelier, in one of the old quarters. Jean-Marc liked the *Marais*, or maybe the *Quartier Latin*. They would eke out a living, he'd work with wood, she would dance (that's what Sandi had done in New York, though at an "adult" club on Lexington and 55th, as the resident transsexual. She didn't confide this to Jean-Marc).

Finally, 'round midnight, they parted miserably, rapturously, at Broadway and 72nd. She would, she whimsically promised, deposit a love letter in a Pepsi Cola bottle at Coney Island, seal it with a kiss, sail it toward France. He would, he said, scour the sea for her testament.

Sandi's last words to Jean-Marc were: "Don't forget to shuttle at Times Square."

Jean-Marc's hotel was on 28th and Madison. And after shuttling at Times Square, he was walking through the tunnel-thoroughfare toward the Lexington Avenue line, when he witnessed a mugging. A boy in sneakers snatched a business-looking-man's attaché case and sailed off through the tunnel. The mugged man spit out his gum and stood there with his mouth open, two or three passengers paused to watch, one of whom, Jean-Marc noticed, was eating French fries from a styrofoam dish.

Jean-Marc had been in New York nearly a week, and to his surprise this was the first mugging he'd seen.

13

RUPTURE

Bordeaux was as it had been, at least in Jean-Marc's relatively brief life: bustling port/vivid sky/vineyards/sea.

And yet nothing was as it had been, since she, Sandi, was not there to share it with him. Scarcely eating, tossing in his bed at night, smoking too many Gauloise Blondes, Jean-Marc thought only of her: fragrant hair, long-nippled small breasts, strong legs, moist full lips, enchanting smile.

Each dusk he would bicycle to the sea, sun going down/tide coming in, and gaze across the ocean in the direction of Coney Island, hungering for Sandi, hankering for her Pepsi bottle. Smiling wistfully, he'd think: stranger things have happened.

As it turned out, Jean-Marc's melancholic longing, an attractive thing in a slender young Frenchman, coincided with the infestation of medical waste that was washing up on the northeast coast of the U.S.

There were the customary accusations, denials, counter-accusations. The fact, simply stated, was that hospitals and clinical labs, after comparing bids, were contracting with the most cost-efficient garbage disposal "systems," which in turn cut costs by doing what coastal industries routinely did: dumped their waste in the ocean.

Not all of this waste washed up in the U.S., some swirled beyond the shore currents and made its way to the Fatherland: Western Europe, who mostly disapprove of us and our thousand points of blight, but that's their problem.

Two weeks, or was it ten days?, after Jean-Marc returned to Bordeaux, he had lost nearly ten pounds, was pining more than ever, cycling to the shore every dusk, gazing like Gatsby across the sea, hoping against hope for a sign, it needn't be in a Pepsi bottle.

He got lucky: something suddenly was bobbing beyond the surf. He removed his shoes, rolled up his trousers to his knees, waded out, the sandpipers scattered. It wasn't a bottle but a bag, plastic, fastened at the top.

Jean-Marc snatched it and made his way back to shore. He sat on a flat rock and lit a Gauloise Blonde. He examined the bag which had the partially effaced words: "Mount Sinai Disp—" on it. He didn't recall that he and Sandi had passed this venerable medical institution on their way to the blackberry bush in Central Park.

He opened the bag and found a smaller bag, opaque and plastic. He opened it and poured the contents on to the rock. It wasn't a love letter. It wasn't a shaved lab rat. It wasn't a batch of bloody syringes.

It was a small section of what looked like viscera. Jean-Marc, who in addition to his refined sentimentality, had something of the aptitude of a clinician (this seeming paradox is not uncommon among the French), did not shrink from his gruesome discovery. He examined it closely under the late fall sun, probing it with his pen, drawing on his cigarette. He concluded, though without certainty, that it was a human penis and fragment of testicle.

MARSEILLES MAFIA

Traditionally, in narratives like this, the pining seventeen-year-old stops pining, resumes eating, goes about his life. While the object of his infatuation undergoes her operation and either dies or loses her faculties through an inadvertent slip of the scalpel. Except that Dr. Lewisohn's scalpel never slips. Like other surgeons in his tax bracket, he doesn't commonly accept Medicaid cases, but he was putting together a book, in fact had received a hefty advance from the publishing conglomerate Macmillan, and Sandi/Santos' situation was clinically noteworthy, even among transsexuals.

"Clinically noteworthy" in what sense, you wonder. I'm not going to say, it is not germane to this text, if your curiosity has not diminished in about fifteen months, consult Dr. Raoul Lewisohn's book, provisionally titled *Transsexual Surgery: Living and Loving in The Real World.*

Less than a week after her surgery, Sandi wrote a long love letter to Jean-Marc, then Xeroxed a copy and slipped it into a Pepsi bottle that she stoppered with a cork. She mailed the letter, and good to her promise, she flung the bottle into the sea at Coney Island.

Afterwards, she and her sister Sonia each ate a world-famous frank at Nathans on the Boardwalk.

Three days after his discovery at sea, Jean-Marc received Sandi's letter, and what a letter it was, filled with the most tender endearments, and best of all she confirmed her intention to come to France, but first she needed to put together some money. She estimated that in a few months, around Christmas time, she would have saved enough to pay her way.

Immediately Jean-Marc wrote to say that he would happily provide Sandi with the necessary fare so that she could leave at once.

Actually Sandi *had* saved enough money for her fare dancing at the adult club on 54th and Lex. But she didn't want to travel until the incision had healed properly, which, according to Dr. Lewisohn, would take at least six weeks.

She wrote to Jean-Marc that she would not feel right accepting such a substantial sum from him at this state of their relationship. And she gently chastised him for wanting to "hurry love." She reminded him that she was older than he (Sandi was nineteen) and that he should accept the "wise advice" of his elder.

Was Sandi nervous about going to Europe (to date, she had not travelled farther than to Puerto Rico), and meeting Jean-Marc's parents?

Not at all: she always got along real nice with people, and she thought of herself as a socially refined young woman. She was nervous only about her surgery. With Jean-Marc she was prepared to do what she had never done: make love like a woman, which is why it was so important for the incision to heal properly.

Would she ever be able to confide to Jean-Marc her sex change? She would cross that bridge when she came to it.

When you are seventeen and French and in love, time, in Bergson's graphic characterization, whirrs by on hummingbird's wings *while* ponderously dragging its length like tripe making its way through Gargantua's digestive tract.

That's Rabelais' Gargantua.

So it was with Jean-Marc who obsessively relived his too-brief passion with Sandi in the Big A while being mired in the endless Bordeaux day. Of course there was school, which technically occupied much of his time, though Jean-Marc had pretty much stopped doing any school work. Instead he played his tapes (Jacques Brel, Tracy Chapman, David Bowie), and wrote verses broadly modeled on Rimbaud: deferred love generating angst. He enclosed these French verses in his letters to Sandi, which were written in painstaking English.

He scarcely ate—he drank coffee and smoked Gauloise Blondes.

His parents, who had learned about parenting in Piaget and Dr. Spock, tried to talk with Jean-Marc, but the young man seemed incapable of coherent response.

Across the sea in Spanish Harlem, Sandi was healing happily while writing tenderly to Jean-Marc three and four times a week. Farther downtown Dr. Raoul Lewisohn was fine-tuning his manuscript preliminary to sending it to his literary agent who would hand-deliver it to the publishing magnate Robert Maxwell's Macmillan. While the Metropolitan Museum of Art was growing richer faster through acquisitions (hostile takeovers), prudent disposal, and diversified investments. While Bernhard Goetz's vigilante chutzpah spawned a virtual industry of Goetz dolls and tie clasps and bumper stickers. While the homeless were metastasizing south and east to Fifth Avenue and Madison Avenue and even Park. While in the world of sports and entertainment . . .

Never mind, I'm just trying to signify passage of time within a realistic narrative framework. Sandi healed and Jean-Marc accumulated verses while physically resembling the knight at arms in Keats's "La Belle Dame Sans Merci": slender wrists, deep eyes, gaunt cheeks. Except that Sandi was merciful and in love and it was Christmas at last and she was flying TWA to Paris, even as Jean-Marc was recklessly rattling in his yellow armadillo Citroën 2CV from Bordeaux to fetch her.

1) Jean-Marc, lighting a Gauloise Blonde, loses control of the wheel of his Citroën and crashes into an embankment outside Limoges, known for its porcelain, dies instantly.

2) Sandi, cramped in economy class, goes to the restroom and while peeing commences to bleed and burn. Something is wrong, she panics, rings for the stewardess.

3) Each arrives intact at Orly, they embrace, collect Sandi's baggage, proceed to Bordeaux, meet Jean-Marc's parents, who politely disapprove, and that night they make love, but there is pain, or something goes wrong, and Sandi tearfully confesses her secret, Jean-Marc is astonished/appalled/chagrined/mortified. Sandi returns to New York on the next available flight.

4) Same as preceding, except the lovemaking is sweet, painless. A fortnight later they leave for Paris, rent a tiny flat north of the *Marais*. Jean-Marc finds work as a messenger in the news room of the *International Herald Tribune*. Sandi works as a seamstress, but the wet Paris winter is seeping into her lungs.

5) Same as preceding, except that once in Paris they rent a flat in the *Quartier Latin*, Jean-Marc finds work as a messenger boy in the copy room of *Le Monde*, while Sandi applies for a job in the Third as a "dancer," which in fact is a cover for a prostitution ring run by the Marseilles Mafia. Sandi resists the oily interviewer's blandishments and huffs out slamming the door. But there are no decent jobs available, and Sandi, depressed, takes to hanging about the tiny flat playing patience. The weather is cold and wet, tension develops between the two lovers, in their misery they abuse each other, finally Jean-Marc slams the door leaving her on the bed, hollow-eyed, coughing.

6) Same as preceding, except that Sandi, after conferring with Jean-Marc, accepts the position of dancer (prostitute), and thanks to her charm and wiles, is soon earning fifty thousand francs a week. But she doesn't lose her head or her love for Jean-Marc; together they bank their francs. After six months they move to a larger flat near Montmartre, get married and Sandi applies for French citizenship. After five years she retires, and with their savings they open a cozy café in the Fourteenth. Coincidentally, the Marseilles Mafia who lured Sandi into prostitution are also into selling protection to shop owners. When Jean-Marc rejects their offer, he is beaten. When Sandi notifies the Gendarmerie, Jean-Marc is murdered and quartered, his parts tossed into the Seine, whence they drift, one attenuated limb finding its way finally to the surf off Coney Island, where it is snatched by a swimmer, a seventy-nine-year-old member of the Polar Bear Club named Angelo, who is surprised by his discovery, though not all that surprised, since these are the lawless 80s.

7) Same as preceding, except that Jean-Marc and Sandi pay the protection and continue to make a profit through thrift, hard work, mutual support and patriotism. Because Sandi can't conceive, they adopt Tunisian twins, one male/one female, the male called Santos, the female Beatrice.

EROS /
Xerox

In the desert between California and Nevada they saw turkey vultures circling and off-the-road vehicles. They saw a California Highway Patrol car that had pulled over an old Chevy, the Latino driver spread-eagled against the hood of his car while the police examined his documents.

They saw born-again billboards and signs prohibiting access to vast sections of the desert in the name of the government. These, they figured, were, or soon would be, nuclear testing sites.

They saw broad-winged hawks against the blue-white sky and here and there a rabbit and one roadrunner and billboards selling Las Vegas.

They got into Vegas at mid-afternoon, drove along the Strip in the direction of downtown, pulled into a motel parking area. Next to the motel was Cupid's Kiss Wedding Chapel, a small gabled structure with a single, tasseled shoe on its side on the roof. Some groom in exultation, or furious regret, must have flung it there after the $50 ceremony.

Checked into the motel and went upstairs to their small room. While she lay on her back in the queen-sized bed smoking a Salem, he raised the blinds and looked out the window which faced a gambling casino. An old woman, her hair in curlers, clutching her purse, shuffled into the casino. Another old woman left. Then two more old women entered, one at a time, they didn't know each other.

He lay in the bed next to her, they kissed.

She switched on the TV with the remote control. The X-rated channel gave you a three-minute preview, after which it cost $6.95 to watch the movie. The preview was of a man and woman fucking without genitals: the cameras kept above their waists.

They switched channels to an old movie that had been colorized. *Dillinger*, with Lawrence Tierney, 1945. Dillinger has mauve eyes, he is lured to the movies by a girlfriend in collusion with the police. The movie Dillinger sees before he is bushwhacked has also been colorized.

Switched off the TV.

On their backs, side by side, they slept. When they woke it was bright outside, but night. She ran a bath and they sat in the small tub facing each other, legs entwined. They shared a Salem.

On the bed again they made love, moving deftly in and out of each other.

They slept.

When they woke it was bright outside and four-twenty a.m. They stood, naked, in front of the window, looking out.

They saw the old woman with the curlers totter out of the casino clutching her purse. She paused in the middle of the street, then turned around and went back into the casino.

They showered, dressed, left, got into their rented car, drove into the desert.

Dawn without the sound of birds.

They saw a hawk dive but come up empty.

They saw the government signs prohibiting access to large sections of the desert, saw the billboards selling Jesus.

They saw a small sign with an Indian name, it pointed northeast into the desert, they turned their car in that direction.

Into the groin of the desert.

They couldn't find the Indian reservation, just more government signs.

Whose government?

Six-fifty a.m. and hot.

They turned onto the main road and saw a CHP car that had pulled over an old Chevy, Latino driver/wife/three young children ordered outside, the driver spread-eagled against the hood of his car in front of his family, the cop licking his fingers while examining the documents.

They drove back into Las Vegas in the early morning and returned to their motel room.

While he lay on his back in the bed smoking a Salem, she looked out the window and saw people, mostly old, mostly old women, going into the casino.

Naked, they lay in bed together. They made love silently.

Made love passionately, silently.

They slept.

They woke in the afternoon in their queen-sized bed in their cramped air-conditioned room. He switched on the TV with the remote control, moving from channel to channel, pausing at a talk show featuring a skinhead with a gun, a Desert Eagle .44 magnum semi-automatic, which was real but unloaded.

Which was unreal but loaded.

Switched off the TV.

The fierce sun penetrated the blinds and gathered in broken lines on the walls and on the bed.

The broken lines are prison bars. And the electronically-generated bars that constitute the TV image. And sex for sale without genitals. And the long uneven border between Mexico and this country. And the plastic curlers in the hair of the old woman in the casino. And the angular shadows of the restricted desert signs in the name of the government. And the ritualized lies of the government. And the sworn revenge in the hearts of the three children witnessing their mortified father spread-eagled on the hood of his car. And the hovering then sudden steep plunge of the hawk that misses or seizes the poisoned prey.

She ran a bath and they sat in the small tub facing each other, legs and arms entwined, both of her wrists and both of his slit, the very red blood reddening the bath water.

EROS/ Exxon

CATECHISM

Whom would you rather love: a woman who does your bidding but is non-orgasmic, or a woman to whom you defer at the expense of your potency, or most of it?

The first, I guess.

How would you rather love: in the "missionary" position with only your bejesus exposed, or naked and polymorphous by the shore of the flooding river?

Flooding river.

What would you rather smell: the sepsis of the terminal

AIDS patients in the warehouse-turned-hospice, or the Eggs Benedict on the colonial china at the prayer breakfast on the Hill?

Sepsis.

What would you rather see: a heron high-stepping through the marsh, or the opportunist's thin lips pronouncing the phrase "thousand points of light"?

The heron.

What do the swastika, Coca Cola, Exxon and Mickey Mouse have in common?

I know that one. They are the canonical images of our epoch.

How would you rather die: in ecstasy that feels like agony, or in a condo that feels like a hospital and you're hooked to electronic monitoring devices?

I don't want to be hooked. You seem to be hooked to this Q & A mode. I know you're enjoying it but it's getting on my nerves.

Sorry.

You get carried away. You don't mean to, I know—

I do mean to.

How's that?

I mean to get carried away. Be carried away. Carry myself away. The principle is: if you can't afflict the technocrat then make yourself delirious.

Why? What good is delirium?

It's a charge, it mimics response.

25

Because "real" response is limited?

Well?

What about withdrawal? A strategic withdrawal?

Where would you rather withdraw to: your condo with its porous walls/radon gas/jackhammers savaging the pavement, or a patch of wilderness which is a game preserve for the truly rich who if they catch you will quarter you?

What about joining them?

Who's that?

The truly rich.

No, that wouldn't play.

Why not? You're full of suet. Your nose is straight, your teeth are capped. A few days of practicing your smile in your shaving mirror and you're ready for prime time.

My nose *isn't* straight, my teeth aren't even white, and what about this gap in front?

Hey, no biggie. I know a dentist, cosmetic guy, he'll plug your gap. And anything else you need. He's down there in Silicon. Telegenics is his specialty.

No, really . . .

Look, I insist. We're pals, right? Okay, we're not exactly pals, but we've downed our share of Bud Light, bullshitted about anabolic steroids and the Marxist incursion in Central America. Now I'd like you to go home, practice your smile in front of your mirror, add a few lights and it's like being on TV. In fact practice your whole demeanor, you've gotten, frankly a little grim-faced in recent months. Think sound-bite/think video-memory. And ditch the negatives, or invest them in junk bonds, because America is moving forward. Talk about the big stick in Israel, in South Africa, Bavaria's renewed prestige, *our* guys will be machoing in their white hats into the next century and beyond: A THOUSAND YEARS OF ROCK AND ROLL.

TEXAS

Hey, you're back.

You still settin' on your duff?

I'm standing. Actually leaning. How about a Bud?

Well, just one. I'm on my way to Tixas.

Texas? What you gonna do there?

See some folks, do some huntin'.

What all you huntin'?

Coon.

That's real in-er-est-ing. How long you figurin' to be there, Texas?

Till Christmas. Comin' back to Anaheim for the holidays.

Sounds good. Sounds darn good. Anaheim's one of the best there is to watch Christmas on TV. There and Texarkana. Also San Ysidro, the American side, where that guy killed all those folks in McDonald's.

Didn't they tear that down? That McDonald's down there?

Yeah, they did. Opened up Blockbuster Video, they're a chain.

Makes real good business sense, don't it.

Better believe it. Whereall in Texas you goin'?

First I'm goin' to Amarillo. Spend a couple, three days at the Desert Marriott down there, prayin'. Then I fly to Dallas/Fort Worth, you know the old Tixas Book Depository building where Kinnedy was killed at? There's talk about razin' it, turnin' the site into a Embassy Row down there.

No kidding? What countries they thinkin' of invitin'?

Well, Japan, of course. West Germany. Also Taiwan, South Africa, Chile, maybe Israel.

What about Waldheim's Austria and the principality of Monaco?

Right. Them too.

Texas goes international, right?

Shoot. Tixas been international for a good long time. Ax folks in the streets in Pretoria, Frankfurt, Tokyo, what have you, to name the first place in America comes to mind, two out of three them say Tixas or Dallas. The Embassy Row thing's just frosting. It's nice, don't get me wrong, but Tixas prestige and stature, what have you, don't depend on Embassy Row.

Uh-huh. 'Nother Bud?

Just one. Like "Dallas" is probably the most popular TV series in recorded history, but that don't mean folks believe everything they see. Take drugs: folks is 'gainst drugs, but they want they barbecue, right? They want they ice-cold beer go along with it. And when they finished, they want they poon—

Wait just a minute! Poon is out and you know it. Women's groups and such like won't stand for it. But coon is in, like you said before, bigger than ever, hatin' 'um/huntin' 'um. Where you think AIDS begun at?

28

Africa's what I heard.

Damn right.

Not South Africa.

No, no way. Zaire, Ghana, Uganda, like that. Zaire used to be called the Congo, maybe you forgot that.

No I dint. I have it written on a index card I keep in my wallet. It's always with me. Alongside the equation that turns Celsius into Farenheit, for when I travel.

What else you have on that index card?

Well, I got me some numbers, escort services and such, but I'm talkin' high-class. Plus they make you use a condom, make double sure.

American-brand condom? The foreign brands tend to burst, you know.

'Specially you shove some Tixas sausage in it.

[Laughter]

SAFE SEX

Good news, Bo.

What you got?

A new hole. They just discovered a new hole. You know, orifice.

What in Jesus' name . . .

Exxon. The research folks at Exxon. Seems they been workin' on it since the AIDS thing. Now it's ready. They perfected it in their labs with test-subject prisoners.

Where's it at?

The lab?

The hole.

In the most convenient place you can imagine: between the anus and the genitals.

What?

You know where the perineum is, right? That's where it's at, the hole.

That's crazy.

No it's not. Least the FDA don't think so.

What do they have to do with it?

Thing is this hole, or orifice, is there in all of us, male and female, and it's basically very sensitive and elastic since it employs the same sphincter action as the anus and the genitals, you see. Just it hasn't been used for eons and eons and so is in a state of disuse. Except for the Essenes.

What?

The biblical Essenes. I guess they were, like, proto-hippies during the time of Jesus. They'd made the discovery of this third hole and were using it in their own sexual congress. Only they were real secretive about it, so the information never really got public. There was, though, one other connection that provided the crucial link to the Exxon researchers. The Masons. Or Freemasons. I forget which one. But they began real early as an outgrowth of the Essenes.

So Exxon infiltrated the Masons.

Exxon did what it had to do, Bo. They were dealing with an epidemic—I'm talking about AIDS—on the order of the medieval plague, the Black Death. Actually, there were two links, both connected with the Essenes: the Masons, like I said, and the Islamic sex adepts. I'm talking about esoteric sex manuals like the Perfumed Garden, the Moslem version of the Kama Sutra. The Exxon researchers discovered in the earliest of these Islamic texts several examples of this third hole being employed. In the later versions these examples were deleted.

Why?

Good question. The Exxon bigs think: pleasure. After the Church Fathers puritanized Christianity and approximately the same thing happened to Islam, there was no place for ecstatic sex separated from the anxiety of disease or childbirth. You see, this third hole is unlike the genitals and the anus in that it is a closed circuit. Though in the throes of sexual congress it exudes a mucusy matter, it—the orifice—does not intersect with either the reproductive system or the large intestine.

Sounds like voodoo physiology.

You've become jaded, Bo. You distrust simplicity. And that's what this is all about: simplicity, congruence. I'll tell you something else: you recall that Exxon was previously known as Esso, in fact still is outside the U.S.? How do you think they hit upon the name: Esso?

It's an anagram of some kind, no?

Obviously. But I'm talking infrastructure, man.

Tell me.

It's as simple as it is elegant: Essene/Esso. [Pause] You needn't look so uneasy. Esso recognized an affinity with the Essenes very early but had to obscure it in accord with what

31

Freud spoke of as the obligatory repression of civilized societies. It is only now, ironically, in the context of the most palpable repression in modern times, that Exxon can revive this crucial, crucial link.

Because of AIDS?

Because of AIDS.

You mentioned the FDA.

Right. The Federal Drug Administration has sanctioned the sale of a product developed by Exxon pharmacologists to dilate the opening of this third hole.

Exxon pharmacologists?

They're diversified, Bo. Lookit, after centuries of virtual disuse, this third orifice naturally atrophied, in some anatomies even became vestigial. The Exxon product conveniently comes in several modalities: injection for fastest acting dilation; liquid drops applied directly to the orifice cicatrix; or capsules ingested between four and eight times daily, depending on the inhabitability of the orifice area.

I can't think what to say except: these products must be very dear, no?

Sure. By ordinary standards they are very dear, but look what all you have to gain?

A third hole.

That's right, Bo. And like I said, it's for females and males. When was the last time you had a foreign member trundling inside *you* without guilt and high anxiety?

You're talking about a transvaluation of values.

I'm talking ecstasy, Bo. Hot shit. From what I hear it will be in the pharmacies by Christmas. It's via prescription, but that won't be a problem: the AMA is keen.

And it's called what—this product? Third Hole?

Not hardly. It's called Exxene.

EROS /
Talk Dirty

I'll call him Rob, he's a software engineer, thirty-six years old and very "manly" looking. We met at one of those corporate challenge races in Central Park, six miles (he finished eleventh out of fifty-eight, I dropped out after the fourth mile with an inflamed Achilles' tendon). Each time I meet an attractive man I envision us as lovers, and the fantasy is intriguing to me. At thirty-three plus, I have had numerous affairs, and I think of myself as a sensual person. After all, I came of age in the roaring sixties, before AIDS, before herpes simplex, before chlamydia.

BUT WHAT DID I REALLY WANT?
AND WHAT DID HE REALLY WANT?

I was fifteen in '69, the summer of Woodstock, but I was an *old* fifteen. Like nearly all the girls I knew then, I got to

revving early, had horsepower to burn, and every day promised another jolt. Sex, drugs, protest marches, tie-dyes, no
bras, Encounter groups, Be-Ins, Happenings: you name it, I
did it.

You know that famous photo of the young girl with the
long blond hair and blissed-out expression sticking a flower in
the barrel of the National Guard soldier's rifle? That was
yours truly, the original flower child.

*And you know who the befuddled Guardsman was, don't you? Vice
president Dan Quayle, the Robert Redford lookalike.*

When I say I was into sex, I mean the kinky stuff, anyway
what would be called kinky now. In those days it was no big
deal: meeting a guy at, say, a peace rally, dropping acid, balling the guy, balling the guy and his buddy, balling the guy and
his buddy and your girlfriend and anyone else who happened
to be there and wanted to get it on. What I'm saying is that
orgies were the coin of the realm in that pastel time.

**I WAS THE ORIGINAL FLOWER CHILD.
KINKY SEX, ORGIES WERE NO BIG DEAL**

Rob, the "manly" software engineer, might have been a
hippie in the sixties as well, I can't say. He grew up, he said, in
Wichita. He didn't talk much about his past, which is not to
say that he did not talk—*that* was the problem.

We made love for the first time after our second date, a gala
deal at the Plaza to honor Bob and Elizabeth Dole's fifteenth,
I think it was, wedding anniversary (the second marriage for
each). The Doles are from Kansas like Rob.

Neither of them could attend but they sent a video wrapped
in red, white and blue bunting, which was projected on a huge
screen to thunderous applause. While Rob applauded he
pressed his thigh against mine and whispered odd—*very*
odd—things into my ear.

When we got back to Rob's apartment (a prestigious ad-
dress on the upper East Side) we were giddy with excitement,
and before I knew it Rob was kissing me like I hadn't been
kissed in a long time: passionately, *personally,* with me thinking dreamily that it not only felt sexy but *right.*

ROB WAS MR. RIGHT? WRONG.

One thing, as the cliché has it, led to another, and soon Rob carried me to his king-sized waterbed and we were in each other's arms, our naked bodies molded together. Sounds romantic, right? Not so fast. While we were still at the Plaza, like I said, Rob would whisper an occasional thing in my ear, sexual stuff, words, dirty words, which struck me as incongruous to say the least, but I was caught up with the Dole festivities, and I had drunk my share of bubbly, so I didn't make that much out of it.

But now in his macho-sized waterbed, beneath his gaudy Hockney repro of the L.A. sweet life, while we were making love, he was *really* talking to me, asking me things: "Does this get you hot?" "Can this get you off?" "Do you like long or short thrusts?" "Do you like the smell of a guy's sweat?"

I thought to myself: maybe he's going through performance anxiety, so I ignored his questions or made vague sounds in response, with the intention of calming his nerves, encouraging him to talk less. It had the *opposite* result, as though my apparent shyness whetted his pornographic appetite.

MY SHYNESS WHETTED HIS PORNOGRAPHIC APPETITE: HE WAS USING ME TO DISPLAY HIMSELF

He got even more specific: "Do you want me to ream your expletive?" "Why don't you stick your expletive in my expletive?" "Should I finger your expletive while I expletive your expletive?" "Will you stick out your tongue while I tongue your expletive?" On and on.

In more years of sexual experiences than I like to admit, beginning in the blissed-out sixties, I've encountered my share of doozies, as you would expect, but this had never, ever happened to me: this dude wasn't nervous, he was sadistic! He was using me to display himself, while my resistance, far from restraining him, was exciting his lurid imagination, getting him off.

36

WHAT KIND OF STUFFED ANIMALS DO YOU LIKE BEST? DO YOU WANT ME TO REAM YOUR EXPLETIVE?

And Rob did not stop with the here and now. He heavy-breathed questions about my underwear: "Do you have a sheer black nightie? Does your nightie get caught in your expletive when you bend down?" "Do you like to wear skirts without panties underneath?" "What kinds of stuffed animals do you like best?" "Do you watch porn flicks?" "Have you ever seen the porn actor Johnny Wadd's thirteen-inch expletive?"

He had pretty good staying power, I'll grant him that, because his weird patter must have gone on for at least half an hour and he was still pumping. But he might as well have had a premature ejaculation, as far as I was concerned, probably that would have been better because I've never been with a man who came too fast who had anything to say for himself beyond some muttered apology.

When I woke the next morning with a champagne hangover on Rob's waterbed, I didn't remember where I was, but then I saw Rob's chalked scrawl on his portable blackboard: JOGGIN', ROB, and I remembered.

How did I feel? Displaced, abused, soiled, ripped off. Ripped off more than anything.

While loverboy was jogging. Jogging and *talking*, no doubt, rehearsing his perverted patter, whispered into the ears of whichever woman he happens to be screwing. Well, it won't be me, not if I can help it. I slid off the bed and into the shower, dressed fast, didn't bother with makeup, got out of there.

FIND A SEAM/PLANT A MINE/SLIP AWAY

Rob phoned daily for the next three days but got my machine. Instead of returning his calls, I made some calls of my own. First I phoned G. J., the leader of the feminist consciousness group that I belong to, and after detailing the entire evening from the Dole festivities to the waterbed, she confirmed every feeling I had—and more. When I mentioned that Rob had carried me to his waterbed, G.J. suggested that there might be grounds for filing a companion rape charge.

I really didn't think I was up to that, but her support buoyed me up. However, my subsequent calls produced very different responses. My roommate from college and my former best friend, who lived on Maui, laughed and said: "Aquarius, count your blessings, you found a live one. Do you realize how many men are stressed-out and impotent or just not interested?"

I admitted that I hadn't really noticed.

Then I phoned another, newer, friend, a high-powered colleague at my brokerage firm. Barb was the kind of woman who wouldn't slip into a pair of pumps in 95-degree weather without first putting on her pantyhose. Barb and I had "done lunch" a few times and I felt that I could level with her. We met at the Quiche 'n Bagel on Third Avenue.

"Barb, do you and Jed [her manfriend] ever talk dirty to each other?"

You can imagine my surprise when Barb paused in mid-bite, flashed her canines in a grin that was positively lascivious and said:

"We sure do, and it's great, just about the best turn on since the invention of the credit card."

What the heck was going on? Had I, Aquarius, flower child, the original "sensuous woman," been somehow left behind?

Was I so caught up in the 80s lifestyle that I had inadvertently allowed myself to become uptight? Stressed-out? A prude?

BRAD WAS A BOGART LOOKALIKE
ATTRACTIVE AND VERY STEADY

I decided to consult still another friend, a male I'd met recently in civil court when I was filing a suit against a Volvo dealership. Brad was an attorney representing the City in a landlord negligence case, and we found ourselves in the same elevator heading to the street level. We had a cup of coffee together in a neighborhood luncheonette and talked.

Brad was forty-three, divorced, a Humphrey Bogart lookalike, but taller, about six-two, and very steady. In fact, attractive as Brad was, there was something about him that inhibited my usual sexual fantasizing.

WE WANT 100 PIECES BREAD,
100 PIECES PEPSI COLA,
THE SKYJACKERS RADIOED TO THE CONTROL TOWER

We made up to meet at three p.m. on Wednesday, in the same neighborhood luncheonette as that first time, and that morning, coincidentally, I was notified by mail that I had won my case against the Volvo dealership and would be receiving a handsome financial settlement. It struck me as a favorable omen.

Brad was waiting for me at "our" table near the window. His tie was loosened and he was smoking a Winston, not holding it between his two longest fingers but between thumb and forefinger, just like Bogart, a little smile on his face. He got up as I approached.

"Oh Brad," I said, and fell into his arms with the tears streaming down my cheeks. But then I regained my composure and pulled away from him.

"I would like you to hear me out," I said. "And then I need your advice."

He nodded and dragged on his Winston.

I started slowly, haltingly, describing my evening with Rob, first at the Dole festivities in the Plaza, then in his apartment, finally in his king-sized waterbed. I found it hard to actually repeat Rob's sexual obscenities, but I forced myself, spelling it all out in the most excruciatingly intimate detail.

FORGET THIS DEVIANT AND GET ON WITH YOUR LIFE

Brad sipped his coffee and smoked, not interrupting, his expression serious but noncommittal. When I finally got it all out, I sighed and had a sip of coffee.

"Is that all of it, kid?"

"Isn't that enough?" I gave him a rueful smile. "What do you make of it?"

He had a pull on his Winston and let the smoke course through his nostrils. "What do *you* make of it?"

"I think Rob's a dangerously disturbed sexual pervert, and I want nothing more to do with him."

Brad was nodding his head, with the tracings of a tender smile on his well-molded lips. "I'm frankly relieved that you feel that way. Because you're absolutely right. Forget about this deviant, kid, and get on with your life."

This simple, straightforward advice was exactly what I needed. I felt so . . . so unburdened. I was staring at Brad with gratitude, my wet eyes wide as saucers.

He picked up his coffee cup and came around to my side of the booth, squeezing down next to me.

"Drink your coffee," he smiled, patting the small of my back.

"Yes, Daddy," I said, giggling.

And that—I suddenly realized—was the first time I had giggled in a long time. I missed giggling, missed acting like a girl, missed being naturally exuberant, instead of relying on the man to initiate the act, the joke, whatever.

I MISSED GIGGLING,
I MISSED ACTING LIKE A GIRL

Well, that was the end of a short lurid chapter in my life, and the beginning of a volume of happiness and security.

Brad and I would announce our engagement the next week, have a church wedding in June, then go off to Haiti for two weeks in paradise and a lifetime commitment to surplus repression.

TWO WEEKS IN HAITI
AND A LIFETIME COMMITMENT TO SURPLUS
REPRESSION

As for sweet-talking Rob, I'm sure that he hasn't experienced much difficulty in finding other women to listen to his filthy patter. P. T. Barnum said a long time ago that "another sucker is born every minute," and unfortunately that applies to women as well, even in this time of feminist awareness. A few of them will even get turned on by Rob's spiel; that is their prerogative. Speaking for myself, in spite of my "Aquarian" background, I am, I learned the hard way, a woman who cherishes the traditional values: family, security, fidelity.

If I were to "talk dirty" with anyone—and I'm not saying I would or could under any circumstances—it would certainly not be with a casual lover, but with Brad, my husband and closest friend.

EROS /
Assault Rifle

RANCHO COSTA

Studying for a test in his Intro class at Rancho Costa J.C., Dale came across the name "Baruch Spinoza" and became nauseous. In the next scene he has graduated *summa cum laude*, is the editor of the Law Review down there at Oral Roberts, and has declared his intention to enter Public Service on behalf of Jesus Hitler and the Pro-Life factions gaining strength throughout the *Hinter* . . . Just kidding, he dropped

out, he's sitting crosslegged on your shag carpet in his jockeys and tattoos field-stripping his gun, a Walther P88, custom, in satin nickel finish with bright gold hammer, Millett sights, scope mount, safety lever, take-down lever, magazine holds fifteen. Skinhead Dale, six-feet-one from snout to

vent, wiry torso, bow-legged from grippin' his Harley, close-together gray eyes, intense, unblinking, bent over his automatic pistol. And what about his assault rifle, AK-47, freshly smuggled out of Comm'nist China, along with a double portion of egg rolls, hold the MSG. *It ain't Dale's fault,* shoot, this gov'ment of ours, it's like being totally absorbed into the sound track of a movie, EAT

SHIT AND DIE KADAFI. It's been proven: when economic pressures mount, people, poor people, colored, start sniping at each other, Hitler makes another comeback on TV. Well at least he ain't the Ayatollah, can you believe that guy, unleashes his shiteaters. Anyways, Dale, he's tard of Toyotas, of beer in the 7-Eleven freezer that he cain't even pronounce the names, let alone afford the price. Well how'd he afford his Walther P88, his

AK-47? He's got him a sugar daddy: a thousand points of light/an estimated seven million homeless, and each light a bunker commanded by a bornagin 'Merican in service to Technocracy's dream of a pink home/green lawn for each and every snub-nosed, thin-lipped hetero-family-of-four-without melanin. I think I'm gone to throw up, ain't that what you *been* doin'?

DALE'S DAY

4:00 a.m.: Nocturnal erection through his jockeys and evil dreams, he's forgetting them as he's dreaming them: somebody is trying to rip the tattoo from his left tricep with a crowbar, the tattoo, homemade, says *MOM* (in real life it says *ZOG*, impaled by a dagger). The "somebody" is dark, a jew, or maybe some kind of mex. Dale tries to get to the Walther in his leg holster, but he can't get under his jeans, but then the assailant, instead of ripping Dale's arm, is pulling at his jeans to get to the tattoo on his left thigh, except what the assailant gets to is his, Dale's, johnson (you know what I'm talkin' 'bout): nocturnal emission/clouds of unknowing.

6:12 a.m.: He's up, he's sticky, his mind's grinding: Who all's he hatin' today, Tuesday? asians, the asian children in the schoolyard, jumpin' around, their mothers with their head-rags, weird, nigger arabs, boat people, they come here, take our

7:15 a.m.: Dale in his tattoos and jockeys in a straight-backed folding chair at the small formica table: instant coffee and the Good Book: the *Turner Diaries,* given to him by the same sugar daddy gave him the P88, AK-47, told him what to do with his johnson keep it from goin' off like it does.

8:40 a.m.: Cross-legged on the floor in his jockeys wiping the oil residue off his AK-47, checking out the ammo.

10:13 a.m.: On his back in his narrow bed counting the cracks in the ceiling: straight cracks 'gainst the crooked cracks: straight cracks is the Green Berets with bowie knives and AK-47s, crooked cracks is the gooks with head-rags, machetes and stolen M16s/talk show on the radio.

11:59 a.m.: Coors and leftover pizza.

1:06 p.m.: Phone rings, wrong number, person has an accent.

1:31 p.m.: Another look at the weapons, field-strips the P88, sticks a patch through the bore: clean, still clean.

2:10 p.m.: Barechested, barefoot, in his blue jeans, on the floor, leaning against the bed, flicks on the TV with the remote, switching back and forth between Aerobics For Pregnant Moms and a sitcom rerun, zipper fly open, flicking his johnson.

2:47 p.m.: Phone rings, picks up the receiver, listens, can hear his own breathing, puts it down, squeezes into his steel-toe Doc Martens, fits the Walther into his leg holster, the AK-47 beneath his camo field jacket, ammo inside big pocket, locks his door, goes downstairs, gets on his Harley, revs, turns to the TV cameras, looks defiantly at the TV cameras into our living room/family room/den, his cheekbones pulsing, his close-together grey eyes clear as agates made pastel by flash floods in the highlands of old Arizona (America loves its good bad boys: Billy the Kid, Babe Ruth, Clyde Barrow, James Dean). Dale pats his thigh, vrooms to the schoolyard.

DALE'S CASE

"When I get up in the morning I say to myself: 'Now I have to go out and catch a man,' and I look at his hands and see he is a working man like myself. And I have to slap him or beat him murderous blows to get him to fear me."
Israeli soldier in the occupied territories

In his Civics class the female teacher played a video of the sixties which went on about this trained ape called hisself King. Dale felt he'd throw up if he didn't get out. He walked out without taking his books, got on his Harley, cut off an old guy in an Audi, damned good car, German engineering. Back to his room on 23rd near the 7-Eleven. Stops off there for some beer and Coke and Spam and two Mars bars and a hundred-fifty watt bulb.

What's he going to do with the high-watt bulb?

45

He's going to screw it into the overhead socket so that when he cleans his guns at night he'll see what he's doing.

You mean when he strips down to his jockeys, sits on the floor cross-legged with his Walther P88 and AK-47 and gun-cleaning gear in front of him, his flat belly, convex navel, long torso, tattoos, telegenic cheekbones, tossing his long straight blond hair away from his eyes—

No, he's skinned, he's a skinhead.

He's a disaffected prole.

Not really. His dad works for HP, Hewlett-Packard, up there in Silicon, in sales. His mom's a legal secretary.

In Silicon Valley?

No, *she's* in Orange County. Anaheim. Near John Wayne Airport. They're divorced.

Dale comes from a broken home?

You betcha.

So what's he have taped to his walls: Playboy bunnies, heavy metal rock dudes?

No. A cutout from the local weekly about how more and more Asians have been immigrating to Rancho Costa. An outsize headline from some skinhead publication about ZOG being responsible for Asians taking American jobs and the consequent stagflation. Another cutout from *Guns and Ammo* about the exceptional "stopping power" of the Walther P88. And a cut-out from the newspaper about that star baseball player messing around: WADE BOGGS: "ADDICTED TO SEX." These items neatly razor-cut, taped on the wall above his sofa bed.

You're saying he *don't* listen to rock, heavy metal, the way some of these whacked-out kids are supposed to do?

46

He listens to talk shows. On TV it's the news, aerobics dancing, maybe a sitcom or game show. Hates MTV.

Why's that?

ZOG. The Zionist Occupational Government has deployed their Jewish entertainment moguls who've gotten state-of-the-art nose jobs from Jewish plastic surgeons to make themselves presentable, then stuck us with MTV, like they stuck us with drugs and fags and runaway inflation. Plus he really don't have an ear for music, Dale.

Girls?

Hard to call. He's not a homo. Seems to get off enough from just jackin' off. Always has that stale spermy smell about him. Have you noticed?

Now that you mention it. What about demonology? We hear that more and more kids, unable to adjust to the rigors of late consumer capital, are into this devil stuff.

What Dale is into is ZOG and their trained apes, Martin Luther Coon etcetera. ZOG gave us fags then gave us AIDS to go along with it. Gave us abortion and drugs and boat people.

DALE ON EYE WITNESS NEWS AT 6

. . . shot at the children, killing seven and wounding eleven others, all Vietnamese or Cambodian. First he emptied his Walther P88, fifteen rounds, killing three and wounding three. Then he used his AK-47 assault rifle, spraying the schoolyard, killing four and wounding eight. The children were all between the ages of five and nine, and when they saw him pointing the Walther they began to run around the schoolyard. They couldn't get out of the yard because the gates were locked, a normal procedure during afternoon recess. A witness at the scene pointed out *this* oddity: though the children were zig-zagging crazily in a futile attempt to evade

47

the gunshots, they weren't screaming, weren't making a sound. The same eyewitness said that Dale walked through the schoolyard holding the Walther in a two-handed grip, arms rigidly extended, turning left then right, with no expression on his face, nailing the kids (they fell lightly, like petals from a tree) like he was practice-firing on the range. By the time the SWAT team arrived and cordoned off the area, Dale had holed himself up in the school basement among the pipes, water beetles, flaking asbestos. Which is where he killed himself, punched a fresh clip into his Walther, stuck the barrel into his mouth and fired up into his palate in the direction of his brain. Splat.

EROS /
Sitcom

When I woke I was in an unfamiliar bed, tightly blanketed, in a wide white room with high ceilings. The far side had ceiling-to-floor drapes in an off-white cotton fabric, but I didn't see a door.

Against a wall was an old portable typewriter on a small metal table, and next to the table on the floor was a TV set, a Philco. I thought they'd gone out of business.

With an effort I squirmed out of the narrow bed and set my feet on the cold stone floor. Actually the floor was not as cold as I expected, and I wasn't sure whether it was stone or some kind of New Age floor covering designed to mimic stone.

Only at that moment, with the word "mimic," did it occur to me that I was wearing pajamas, though I always slept in the raw, as you would expect from someone who entitled his eccentric network of tales *EROS*.

Not just pajamas but silk, or simulated silk, pajamas, and bright orange, like the color of a VW Beetle I once had that constantly betrayed me. I twisted around the collar: Brooks Brothers. Now that was a joke, I'd never buy anything from those proto-yuppies with their pretentious and faintly revolting logo of the Golden Fleece.

I bought all, or nearly all, my goods from catalog outlets like Bean and Orvis and Banana Republic and Lands' End. Had I ever bought a single item from Brooks Brothers? I scratched my head (the left, thin-haired side) to jog my memory.

Well, once, just once, to play a joke on a girl I was sleeping with, I purchased a pair of red ant boxer shorts from Brooks Brothers on Madison Avenue in New York. The joke was that she had labeled me a macho briefs-man, jockeys.

How did the joke go over? So-so. The loving went over better, with her it was dynamite loving, always. She had the more or less improbable name of Rhoda, I called her Ro.

The odd thing, the particularly improbable thing, is that the red ant boxers caper marked the last time we made love. I joined the National Guard, like Dan Quayle, to serve my country. While Ro married a fledgling dentist and moved to Miami (this was before Castro unleashed his sickos and sullied that city, pink and white).

Never mind all that.

How did I get here and what was I going to do? First I glanced at the typewriter (with a sheaf of bond alongside it), then at the TV. No contest: I switched on the TV with the remote control that was on the floor near the bed.

It was a cable hookup, a bunch of channels: one showing aerobics for pregnant mothers, two "reporting" business news, with the stock quotations ticking off on the bottom of the screen, there were several game shows, about as many cartoons, and three or four televangelists, though one of these, gap-toothed, with a wide grin sutured on his face, may have been selling Real Estate.

Then there was a grainy black and white repeat of some sitcom or other. I was about to press "channel" when something struck me: the image of the young man applying Old Spice to his cheeks preparatory to going on his date had mildly askew features and deep-set eyes. His dark hair was thick and wavy and combed back in a "ducktail."

What was he wearing?

He was barechested (the fine hair on his chest trailing a thin line to his navel), *and he was wearing red ant boxers*. My God, I am watching myself en route to swivel-hipped Rhoda and our fateful lovemaking.

Immediately I realized this, there was a break and commercials, a baker's dozen, all in black and white: Pepsi, Clearasil, Joy dishwashing cleanser, Kent cigarettes, Modess sanitary napkins, The A & P supermarkets, Bayer aspirin, Chef BoyArDee . . .

When the sitcom came back on, something was wrong: the young guy was not with Rhoda, or maybe he had been with her and they cut that scene to fit in all the commercials. He was with his buddies in a car, a Chevy Impala convertible. They exchanged the usual dumb jokes while playing to the cameras. Every time they mugged, which meant about every time they opened their mouths, the laugh track shot on with a moronic roar.

The terminus of their drive was a diner, and now they clustered restlessly around the white formica table nursing their shakes while exchanging jokey put-downs and making faces.

And now I couldn't distinguish myself, my young self, from the others, which wasn't the way it had been: I was always different.

I switched off the TV and sat down at the typewriter (an old Olivetti Lettera 22). I rolled a sheet of paper into the carriage and wrote: "He imitates his subjects in order to insert the crowbar of his hate (love) into the finest joints of their posture."

I got up. I was fooling around with the TV and the typewriter and I had no idea where I was or how I got there. Again I looked around the room, and this time I noticed a small reproduction tacked onto one of the walls, fairly high: Van Gogh's *Prisoners at Exercise*, from his Saint-Remy period: twenty-odd sallow, slouch-shouldered men in prison livery walking round and round in a circle in a closed stone space, only one face—Vincent's own, clearly—daring to look out accusingly at the spectator, as if to say:

Why this prison?
Why the larger prison?
Why the imprisonment of the passions?

You can see that I was familiar with Van Gogh's oil, in fact it was one of my favorite paintings, if I could apply "favorite" to such a personal testament.

Virtuous Vincent, who aimed the gun at his heart and missed, but died just the same, after a while, lying on his cot facing the wall. Not even Theo could help.

Theo "helped" by dying himself, within months of his brother's death.

R.I.P. Vincent/Theo.

What should I do now?

I pulled the rope to open the drapes, but instead of a window there was a fresco on the continuation of the white wall: generic, swarthy peasants leading their cattle while gesticulating. One of the heifers had its head turned up (this bit of modeling was clumsy), maybe lowing at the sky. Bottom right, hanging back, were a pair of youthful lovers, the maid with her head lowered, the swain making eyes. What was the point of it?

If the fresco was meant to impress me, why not Diego Rivera, with his moral courage and physical passion and girth and charm and cunning?

Formulating these attributes of Rivera seemed to wake me up decisively, and I was pissed. Who would care enough about me to imprison me? And if they granted me Van Gogh in prison, why did they tack on the sappy fresco? And why the silk pajamas when anyone who really knew me would have to know that sleeping in the nude in any weather was, for me, an article of faith, especially when, at middle age, I commenced to write about physical love.

I switched on the TV again: the sitcom in black and white had given way to the Pentecost in color: a silver-haired televangelist with dyed black beard and fat waist, white on white shirt, custom suit/gold tasseled loafers. He was clasping the hand of his Mrs.: a Tammy Faye lookalike, with pink teased hair, femme-fatale mascara and a purple fist of rouge on each cheek, wearing an agglomeration of lace, frills, crinoline . . .

I pressed the remote and, oddly, got the sitcom on another channel. Once again he stood in front of his bathroom mirror in his red ant boxers from Brooks Brothers applying the Old Spice. I could smell the Old Spice and I remembered Lumumba and J.F.K. with his outsize libido and bad back and Wilt Chamberlain scoring 100 points in an NBA game (against the, then hapless, New York Knicks).

A bit of bandaid for the shaving cut on the chin, which served the dual purpose of obscuring a pimple. Turning the key in the door: top key to the left, bottom key to the right. And I'm off, humming a sexy something from *West Side Story*, already hard, or semi-hard, thinking of Ro's response to my red ant boxers. She has a sensitive tongue, very pink, and soon enough she is playing the game: bending her head (long graceful nape), licking the red ants, giggling, gazing up at me with one large brown radiant eye.

Where her parents?

Well, her mother is with the "girls" playing Canasta, while her father is watching the Yankees on TV in the living room. It is the miracle season of '61 with Maris and Mantle homering about every day, I like Maris especially, his introversion. We're in Ro's room, her door closed but unlocked.

We're lying side by side on the carpet, me in my comical shorts, Ro slim and pink and naked, she is laughing, displaying her long pink tongue. I am (this is noteworthy) relaxed . . .

Commercials: a senior executive from Esso.

Hold the phone! Esso preceded Exxon, which has been with us now for at least twenty mega-profitable years, right? So what goes here? The other channels are in color and up-to-date. Only this one, the sitcom, with its fool's armor of commercials, is stuck in '61, when Black Africa was in a stroke (that's how it was presented) freed, with its sudden plethora of comical (to us) names: Lumumba/Kasavubu/Mobutu/Tshombe.

What happened?

Well, the CIA, scheming with the Belgian right, excised the best of them: Patrice Lumumba.

I switched off the TV.

I can think systematically, am even rather good at it, but I don't do it as a rule, and it was only now that it occurred to me that since the room had neither door nor window how did I get in it?

Do you like Edgar Poe?

I like Edgar Poe, every "cerebral" writer must like Edgar Poe, but I don't share his hypothetical paranoia. I have a sort of reputation, I've made enemies and friends. I have what Freud called an anal-expulsive personality, which means, I think, that I've loved and loathed with considerable velocity. I've often wished I was more equable, more like other citizens, like the version of me in the sitcom, mugging and jiving with my pals in the Impala/at the diner . . .

The point is: I can't imagine who could have designed this "torment" for me. Quotes around torment because I can think of worse sufferings, locking me in a suburban shopping mall with patriotic home owners, for example.

I pressed the remote, the sitcom came on, and again the crucial lovemaking had been bypassed, and now we were in "our diner" (not the same diner as in the banal buddies scene), *après sex*, having coffee and what used to be called, and maybe still is, pound cake. Ro has that familiar satisfied-loving gleam in her brown eyes, and so must I. No, my expression is noncommittal. I remember: Ro is about to tell me that she'd like us to marry, but that if I chose not to, as she suspected, she would accelerate her interest in the fledgling dentist referred to above.

I am on the horns of a dilemma, which is better than wearing horns, but is bad enough given that I don't want to give up the sweet sex, but I certainly don't want to get married. I'm only twenty-one, Ro is nineteen, though I love making love with her, I don't, I think, love her for the long haul, if I can put it that way.

Now she is nodding her head, the light is gone from her eyes, replaced by a realpolitik look, as if to say: "I'm sorry you feel that way, now I'll set about doing what I have to do."

But had she even made love with the dentist? Could she have enjoyed his loving as much as mine? I didn't ask her. That was the last time we saw each other.

My God, who cares? It was nearly thirty years ago and now the commercials are back. I switch off the TV.

But now I have a hard-on, in my bright orange silk pajamas, Ro still has that effect on me, even mediated by the ratty Philco. *O Technology. O Humanity.*

And what a gorgeous hard-on it is, but what good was it? I felt, for the first time, claustrophobic. The room was, as I said, wide/white/high, and it wasn't airless, somehow. It was my impotent hard-on that brought on the claustrophobia.

Why *wasn't* it airless? I looked carefully at the floor and still couldn't decide whether it was real or pastiched (so to speak) stone. Next I tapped the white wall, which seemed to be of plaster with an infrastructure of stone or, anyway, a solid amalgam. Then I carefully scanned the ceiling and saw in the far corner, above and to the right of the heifer lowing at the sky a small grated opening, which must be a vent.

If this were Edgar Poe, a virulent gas would at this instant issue through the vent. But I've already written about gas in "Eros/Exxon" (op. cit.), and besides none of my enemies know I'm Jewish. Or do they? It is never a good idea, as R. Nixon well put it in *Six Crises*, to underestimate the ingenuity of your enemies.

Clarification: I'm Jewish, like Norman Mailer, by birth, I can't help that, maybe it's penance for insufficient lamenting in a former life, but I'm a Mugwump, I've written about *both* Kristallnachts, the first in 1938 in Germany, this one in '88 on the West Bank, shattering bones with rubber bullets, demolishing homes with dynamite.

I'm a crypto-Buddhist, pledged to honesty, and I'll pull out every stop to honor that pledge, knowing all the while that the Zeitgeist has deprivileged honesty/sincerity/authenticity. I am—you surely see it—all those admirable adjectives, I mean nouns, which must be why I've been done to this way: *Edgar Poe.*

I moved the chair beneath the small ceiling opening and got up on it. Geez, my hard-on was getting in the way, yes, I still had it and it was bugging me that I'd have to waste it. *What would Norman Mailer do?* He wouldn't jack off, we know that. He wouldn't drive his "tiny fist" (Gore Vidal's generous phrase) through the wall, even with his karate training— probably you don't know this about N.M., it coincided with his relatively brief CIA phase, enough said.

Anyway, I'm six-feet-two-plus and I couldn't reach the ceiling standing on the chair. I got down, removed the Olivetti from the table, which was taller than the chair, set it beneath the ceiling opening, and climbed on top. It was somewhat rickety, which irked me, how was I supposed to type efficiently on a rickety table?

In any case, even standing on my toes on the table, I was unable to reach the ceiling with my hand. And now my hard-on was gone. I climbed off the table and sat in the chair with my head in my hands feeling very disconsolate . . .

How long can you sit with your head in your hands? I switched on the TV to channel 8 which ten or fifteen minutes ago (there was no clock in the room) was showing the black and white sitcom. Now it was back to the televangelist with the long thin nose, in color, dyed beard/fat waist, and now his wife was weeping, evidently for joy, her mascara was making a mess.

I pressed the remote: the sports channel, which earlier had been broadcasting "News from Wall Street," was televising a bowling tournament, *live*, from Cedar Rapids, Iowa.

I found the sitcom on 14: I am in my National Guard uniform standing with my back against a whitewashed wall, my father is snapping a photo of me, I have an odd expression on my face: strained, numbed. I remember that it unnerved me that my father was proud of me in my uniform, though I could never evoke a response from him when I did something that mattered to me, like publishing a poem in the college magazine. But that's an old and familiar tale, no?, written and joked about by Jewish comics on and off the Borscht Circuit.

And now I am in my uniform walking the streets of what looks like Spanish Harlem. Yes, 111th and Madison, I recognize one of the large bodegas. What am I doing there? I can tell by my odd lurch that I'm feeling lonely and looking for companionship (here I have to compliment the young TV actor: his duplication of my preoccupied lurching gait is the best bit of mimicry since Belushi did Joe Cocker on *Saturday Night Live*).

I found what I was looking for, almost, a Puerto Rican girl of about eighteen, three or four months pregnant. Holding hands, we walked down to Fifth Avenue and sat on a bench looking up into the windows of the wealthy high above Central Park. I don't think we made love, where could we have?, then again it was late, we could've spread newspapers on the cold floor of a deserted subway platform.

Platform gave me an idea (I don't think quickly about mechanical problems): I got up and arranged the chair *on top* of the table, stepped back, appraised this unit, and reflected somewhat morosely.

I've always been athletic, or reasonably so, but I have long thin (though shapely) legs and what is called a high center of gravity. So that climbing on top of the small wood chair which was balanced precariously on the rickety metal table presented certain problems. Fortunately my erection had receded, so at least that wouldn't get in my way. If only there was something to hold on to. What would Norman Mailer do? *He would never have permitted himself to get sucked into this kind of predicament.* He is a much smaller man than Hemingway, but don't, please, underestimate him. He never, or rarely, exposed his flank. And he was a hell of a cocksman in his time. Sure, he's become more conservative in recent years, but that can be attributed to increased age, fatter and fatter contracts and a baker's dozen of marriages and romantic "alliances." Never mind Mailer.

I actually managed to climb up on the small chair and was extending my body to its full height when I shouted, startling myself, and I toppled onto the stone floor after bruising my knee on the table edge, the chair falling on top of me. Except for my knee which was bleeding a little, I was unhurt.

But why did I shout? No, it was the "me" in the TV sitcom, which I had left on. I had contracted gonorrhea (in New Jersey not Spanish Harlem), and the army nurse (male) was, none too delicately, drawing blood, and because he was contemptuous, inept, and, as I recall, a patriot, he couldn't find a vein, and in a final unreasoning assault jammed the needle into my arm, and I shouted, toppling me from my perch.

I reached for the remote and switched off the TV, noticing at the same time that I'd also hurt my elbow in the fall.

What now?

Do it again.

The second try was chancier than the first because of my injuries, but I concentrated (one of my half-dozen virtues was that, like Mailer and R. Nixon, I was usually able to focus my energies in crises). I straightened my body, extended my arm, splayed my fingers, and still missed reaching the ceiling by three or four inches. *Merde!*

Still, I could see that it was in fact a vent, projecting slightly from the ceiling. I could even feel, vaguely, an issue of air.

I climbed down carefully, sat on the bed, and observed for the first time that except for a small desk light fitted into the wall near where the typewriter table had been, there was no electric light in the room. And yet there was light, or light enough: except for writing/reading, my eyes do not want much light.

Nor (and this will have already occurred to the pragmatic American reader) was there a toilet in the room. However, there was a metal bucket (I should have said this earlier) which was obviously a kind of chamberpot. Which I used now, without hesitation, peeing long and languorously.

How could I feel anything even remotely like languor in this predicament? I can't tell you. In spite of my ability to concentrate during crises, I'm not really a grace-under-pressure guy. Truthfully, I tend to panic under pressure, at least initially. I don't like unexpected "problem-solving," but as the crisis continues/ripens/festers, I warm to it, cool off, concentrate.

Anyway, the piss felt good, but it ended as all things, excepting everlasting damnation for communists and eternal Johnny Walker Black Label for fat-waisted televangelists, must.

Now it was back to problem solving. The advantage, for me, was that there were few options, and I always preferred a spare canvas: unaccompanied cello, three-ball billiards rather than the multi-balled, multi-pocketed kind.

Oddly, I felt like writing, but it seemed an effort to move the table and chair and set up the typewriter. Writing what? I don't know, I don't usually know until I do it (this apparent privileging of the imagination is now in disrepute among the French-accented theorists, still it worked that way for Basho/Rimbaud/Keats/Dostoyevsky/Woolf/Artaud/Van Gogh/Mahler (not *Mailer*), and it still does despite our being sucked into the maelstrom of image-glut, commonly called "information").

With typing out, at least for the moment, I could either nap, masturbate (though not with the incubus of an intensely gesticulating Mailer), or watch TV. I reached for the remote.

Surprise: the sitcom featuring the youthful me was still on 14, but again it had jumped back and was now in the Impala convertible en route to the diner. Far be it for me, of all people, to champion realism and verisimilitude, but this business with the banal buddies playing the dozens and grandstanding had nothing at all to do with the youthful me. Reconstitute me if you like, but don't strip me of my isolation/exile/deterritorialization.

I switched channels: the televangelist's wife had tears in her eyes but was no longer weeping, at least for the moment, her mascara was repaired, she was listening to a guest (though imagining herself), himself a televanglist, from the hills of Orange County, singing a hymn while playing the piano, Jimmy Swaggart style, though without Swag's occasional funky syncopation. (Did you know that Swaggart and Jerry Lee Lewis are kin?)

I switched off the TV and lay back in bed. I closed my eyes and felt a tug in the area of my fly, beneath the orange silk pajamas, I ignored the tug: if I jacked off now I would lose the djinni services of Norman Mailer, and, too, I wouldn't be able to jack off later. I'm vigorous, still it takes time to bounce back, this is not '61 and Ro bouncing as she walked. Once I was standing on my roof, taking the sun (tar beach), when I saw her walk by three stories below, she didn't see me. I watched her, moved by the way she moved, she was wearing light-weight denims, the rhythm of her hips guiding her, we were already lovers, I went downstairs to my room, didn't phone her, masturbated powerfully. I saw her that evening, didn't tell her I'd watched her, we made passionate love. Yet what remains with me now is the solitary jack-off.

Which now, I commit again, pace Mailer.

Where am I? I must have dozed. Right. To my more fastidious, or hygienic, readers: I didn't jack off onto the floor but into the chamberpot, only twice outgunning the metal bucket.

Do you know Peter North, the porn-video star? He could squirt you in the eye with his peter from across the room.

And so could I, in my day.

I'd like to see Mailer or Swaggart or Nixon or Waldheim or any of 'em match that.

I had an idea, which must have come to me while sleeping, like Edgar Cayce, a fruitful time for me. It was: set the chair on the table and the TV on the chair, climb on top of the TV, reach up to the vent in the ceiling.

I unplugged the TV and carried it to the other side of the room, an old Philco, as I said, and a heavy sucker. I'm not weak, in fact I'm strong, fundamentally, but I have an incipient, if that's the right word, hernia, which flares up when I lug things.

Well, I got the chair on top of the table and the TV on top of the chair. Now if only I were Chinese, an acrobat with short supple limbs and a low center of gravity. Of course, short limbs would prevent him/her from reaching the vent. So there is something good to be said about not being Chinese, after all.

My own elongated limbs were somewhat stiff from my nap, I supposed, and from my previous effort. But I concentrated and actually managed to get on top of the Philco, which with its old-fashioned metal casing, easily held my weight. In this way I was able to reach the ceiling with both hands. With my right I held the ceiling for balance, while with my left (I'm left-handed in case you didn't guess), I reached up into the vent, actually a metal (or metal-mimicking) grate or grid, like miniature bars in a cell, and projecting slightly down from the ceiling, as though in relief. I pulled, then pushed, then pulled again as hard as I could, nearly losing my balance. It was immovable, didn't give at all. I stopped tugging and pushing and held my hand to it: I could feel, very faintly, air circulating.

What if I shout? Amazingly, that was the first time I even thought of shouting for help/succor/sympathy. And even now I hesitated. Why? You could hardly expect me to analyze *why* while stretched as if on the rack.

Anyway, I gave in and shouted, but I couldn't get myself to pronounce the word "help," so I shouted *Yo* and repeated it: *Yo-ooo*, getting into the spirit of it, though still not without self-consciousness.

Finally I shouted the talismanic MAILER, repeating it several times, to no effect. Either the name had, in the process of accumulating lucre, lost its luster, or my tormenter was simply not tuned in to literary society. Well, I couldn't stand on top of the Philco all day, could I? As I climbed down, something occurred to me: wrap the TV's electric cord around the grate for more pull and leverage. But what if the cord broke?, then I wouldn't be able to watch TV, which would mean that my sole outlet, if that's the right word, would be the typewriter, or maybe more shouting.

Pause for analysis: The reason I couldn't shout heartily through, or into, the grate, has nothing to do with my sometime inability, or disinclination, to shout out, or sound off, at the moment of sexual release. It, my not shouting full-throatedly through the grate, has to do with my not believing this, whatever it was, was happening to me: writer, educator, exile, closet-Buddhist, sports fan, sexy fellow, fruitful dreamer/ fruitless schemer . . .

Right. I dismantled the unit beneath the vent, set the TV on the floor, plugged it in, switched it on. The sitcom was no longer on 14, which was now a "shopping channel," a blond young woman, with sculpted cheekbones and pronounced overbite, at a table encompassed by Disney objects in clay or china: a Goofy spitoon, a Minnie ash tray, Bambi Ben-Wa balls, a Pinocchio mustache cup . . .

I found the sitcom on 23, and there I was: demobbed, dismissed medically from the National Guard on account of asthma. It *wasn't* gonorrhea after all, but asthma mimicking the symptoms of gonorrhea, or so the tests in the vet hospital indicated.

I was walking down the streets of New York (First Avenue in the Fifties, I could make out the Queensboro Bridge), looking contented, though a bit preoccupied and maybe horny. Where was I going? To an assignation (Edgar Poe) with a young black woman named Cohen, adopted as she explained over cappuccino in the Peacock Cafe, when it was still on West 4th Street, by a Jewish family in Jackson Heights, Queens, who called her Joan. Joan Cohen.

We'd emerged (though not together) from the Bleecker Street Cinema after seeing *Last Year at Marienbad*, both of us walking west on Bleecker, not so much walking as drifting or gliding, still under the sway of Resnais' sentimental cubism.

Anyway, I saw her in front of me, attractive with her preoccupied long-legged lope, her hair bouncing rhythmically with each stride, I overtook her, we talked, then stopped at the Peacock. She did most of the talking, pitching from one thing to another: French cinema, her stepmother's mood swings, the "sexy" streetworkers (they were re-piping Sullivan Street), sewing (she sewed her own clothes), the difficulties of growing up Black and Jewish in Jackson Heights, so on.

She'd asked nothing about me, didn't seem particularly attracted to me, and I had decided to write it, or us, off, so far as sex partners went, when, after I'd paid the bill, she invited me to her apartment on Horatio Street.

But then, walking north on West 4th, she remembered, she said, that her roommate was "entertaining," and so it would be better the next day, when she'd have the apartment to herself.

So it is, then, that I am watching the clever actor duplicate my walk (less lurch at this juncture, more stride), my abstracted but anticipatory, even foreboding, walk in the direction of Joan Cohen.

As it turned out, foreboding was accurate, but here come the commercials, and not wanting to relive the misspent afternoon with Joan Cohen, I switch off the TV and sit down at the Olivetti (replaced on its metal table).

I'd already written: "He imitates his subjects in order to insert the crowbar of his hate (love) into the finest joints of their posture." To that I added: "Joan Cohen was virtuous. Joan Cohen was frigid. Joan Cohen lived uneasily in several worlds, each encroaching on the other, so that she never inhabited a single space. She understood this, even joked about it, but since she couldn't expiate it by dramatizing it (as I, for example, can), it ate at her, killed her. Joan Cohen killed her self/selves. Where was I? Offstage. Interested enough to phone her occasionally. What sort of interest? Well, sexual, in part. The terrible tension in her pulled her in the direction of "strange" sex, which she felt she owed herself, despising herself. I saw this, and while feeling for her felt too the sexual tug. Was that all? Well, we did meet, more or less by chance, a few weeks, or months, after the second time I saw her on that fruitless afternoon. She invited me back to her apartment, her roommate gone, in truth there had never been a roommate, just her unmated selves . . . "

But here the typewriter ribbon had run down. I checked it: an old black and red ribbon which had already been turned over once, and now was about finished on the other side.

Talk about insult. More than the silk pajamas and rickety table and banal fresco: why *supply* the funky shit-spouting Olivetti if I can't type with it? A not-so-oblique commentary on my potency as a writer? For the first time I felt depressed.

I know I said earlier that I had felt "disconsolate," but depressed is different, and worse, believe me.

Do you want me to anatomize depression? I would have you sitting on the edge of your seat nervously biting your cuticles. On the other hand, Graham Greene, who understands, as he's frequently claimed, women, insists that they, the distaff side, do not find depressed men attractive, irrespective of how far they can squirt their jizz.

"Jizz" for some reason inclined me to look down at the table, where I noticed for the first time a drawer, in which I found an old-fashioned rubber eraser, one side for pencil, the other for pen, a small wooden ruler, and a spare typewriter ribbon, red and black.

So now the conflict was: change the ribbon and filthy your fingers, or switch on the TV? I ruled on the side of disciplined compulsion and set about changing the ribbon, blackening my fingers and no place to wash. If my tormentor was civilized enough to supply a chamberpot, why not a pitcher of water and basin?

Now and again I phoned Joan Cohen, as I said, but had she ever phoned me? What about those calls I'd get 'round midnight, the caller hanging up as soon as I picked up the phone? Then, after a dozen or so of these calls on successive, as I recall, nights, the phone rang at midnight and it was Joan Cohen.

"What are you doing?" she asked.

"Now? Talking to you."

"The phone is by your bed?"

"Yes."

"So you're lying in bed. You're lying on your back?"

"Uh huh."

"What are you wearing?"

I saw where this was going and let Joan orchestrate our mutual masturbation.

Hang on, the ribbon's twisted. And I'm not much good with my hands . . .

When did this happen, the phone thing, in relation to her, Joan Cohen's, suicide?

I pushed the chair away from the table. Yet again I'd allowed myself to forget my imprisonment, gotten caught up in this fiction of Joan Cohen, who, like me on my Philco/chair/ table, was tottering, as it were, looking for the outlet, the out.

I sat on the bed, switched on the TV: "Aerobics for Seniors" in progress, from "Hollywood West," Honolulu, Hawaii. Senior defined as 45 and over. I got up and tried to follow the exercises, but all that jumping around in my silk pajamas gave me, believe it or not, a hard-on.

How, you're thinking, could a "senior" who is locked in a white windowless room without food or proper toilet facilities get all worked up sexually that way?

I don't know. Consider: is this enforced seclusion really worse than living "in the world"? As for food, the fact that my tormentor had not provided any hadn't occurred to me until just now. Luckily, I wasn't the type who often got hungry. Though it would be nice to have a cup of coffee, or cappuccino.

My erection had receded, but I switched channels anyway: a televangelist with stick-out ears was standing in front of a large map of the world with his pointer on Texas and his eyes closed, evidently in prayer. Texas, on his map, looked as big as the continent of Africa.

The sports channel left bowling and was now doing "equestrian," the straight-spined gentility guiding their mounts over obstacles. The shopping channel was featuring gold-plated jewelry ornamented with gold-plated miniature body parts: slender fingers; a muscular arm; cutesy child's toes; an almond-shaped eye with long, gold lashes . . .

As you can see, I am hesitating about switching to the sit-com, but finally I give in, and coincidentally Joan Cohen has just phoned: I am lying on my back on the bed. (The TV director employs the split screen to convey Joan and the actor impersonating the youthful me):

"What are you doing?"

"Now? Talking to you."

"The phone is near your bed?"

"Actually it's on my bed, along with me."

"So you're lying in bed. What are you wearing?"

"You got me out of the shower. So all I have is a towel. It's blue and not very large."

"It can't cover all of you, can it?"

"No, Joan."

"I like the way you say: 'No, Joan.' "

"Well, where are you and what are *you* wearing?"

"Me? Are you asking about me?"

"Yes."

"I'm laying—or is it lying?"

"I don't care."

"On the rug on the floor, the Indian rug, do you remember it?"

"I think so."

"That's where I am, in front of the radiator, I'm on my left side holding the phone in my right hand, and I'm nude."

"I think you mean 'naked.' "

"Why? All right, naked."

The sound of breathing, no words.

"Do you like the shaved look?" from Joan Cohen.

"Shaved look?"

"I've just shaved my pussy."

Pause.

"How come?"

"I don't know. I like the smell of the lavender aftershave I use. And some men like the look. What about you?"

"Me? Well, that depends. I'd have to see it to know if I liked it, wouldn't I?"

"No. Listen to me. Move the fingers of your left hand . . . "

But here we break for a chamberpot of commercials. In the meantime you wonder how it is that American TV, as prudish about sexual candor as it is wanton about sexual coyness could possibly display Joan Cohen shaved and fragrant alongside (via the split screen) me, naked/buoyant.

I can't answer that.

Ask my tormentor.

I switched off the TV, feeling suddenly hungry, weary, irritated. And, yes, a little bit horny. But what's the use? With Joan Cohen it was all game-playing, herself at the controls. I could get into it once in a while, but mostly she, Joan, annoyed and frustrated me then, as she's doing now.

I shouldn't, I know, speak harshly of the dead, and I wish it had been different, the youthful me with his head by her lavender-sweet lips.

The head of his head . . .

Did I say that one of the first things she asked me was was I circumcised?

I said what difference did it make?

She said her sexual fantasies were of uncircumcised men, though she could never, as she put it, love one.

Got to be, finally, too much. Either I didn't answer the phone (this was before answering-machine technology) or I hung up on her.

Once, as I was about to say for the 50th time that I couldn't talk, she put it to me with disarming plainness:

"But what is it? What's wrong with me?"

I said, after hesitating: "There's lots that's wrong with you, Joan. And I'm helpless to do anything about it. I'm sorry."

And that ended it. I saw her once more in the Village, on Christopher Street, near Hudson, where I'd gone to buy coffee. She cut me, walked right by as if she didn't know me.

A few weeks later, more or less, I can't tell you exactly, she was gone.

How? I was hoping you wouldn't ask me that. Not the way females tend to kill themselves, which is, as I understand it, by pills or slitting their wrists. Joan Cohen hanged herself.

I switched off the TV. Or did I switch it on?

I pushed away from the table, or had I done that already?

I lay on my back on the bed and closed my eyes and pined for a cup of cappuccino and damned my tormentor, and while pining and damning I had a vision: employing the drape cord (do you recall the drapes that protected the fresco?), I would slip it through the vent and as a fitting, or congruent, expiation of my role in Joan Cohen's suicide, I'd hang *myself.*

First, though, I switch on the TV. Sure enough, the young actor is no longer particularly young, the "aging" achieved, somewhat crudely, by makeup. In any case, he's come to the end of the line, and in a room that is white and wide (though with a window facing an institutional highrise instead of my Italian fresco), he is, with the aid of the drape cord, about to end it. Only here come the commercials . . .

I compel myself to watch them, or at least not to switch channels, and after six or seven minutes the sitcom returns, and now I have once again set chair on table and balanced the TV on top of the chair. It occurs to me that it might be steadier to stand on the metal chamberpot than on the TV, but then where would I empty the slops?

So it is the Philco on which I am once more uncertainly balanced, the drape cord in my hand (still attached to the drape, since I have no knife with which to free the cord). The cord is braided and somewhat thick, whereas the space between the vents is narrow, and as I am not a mechanical man, I am having trouble. But thanks to the miracle of technology, the next thing the audience knows I have the cord draped around the vent and am fitting my head through the "noose," but here comes another problem: I have a very large head, size 7 and 7/8ths, and I've fashioned the noose too small. Meanwhile I'm poorly balanced with my knees bent in my orange silk pajamas on top of the Philco, and—you won't believe this—I've gotten still another erection. It must be the silk, or maybe the complex allure of death, but again technology intervenes: the erection is voided and I am fitting my head through the noose, thinking: Joan Cohen, save me a spot in heaven, or hell for that matter, it couldn't be much worse than this white wide room with its banal fresco and Philco TV and Olivetti typewriter.

Here goes: I sort of jump out, the Philco goes tumbling and so does the chair, I hear a roar, like the rush of surf, and I'm on the stone (or simulated stone) floor with the table and drape *and the vent* on top of me encompassed by laughter. And I too am laughing, staring up into the black hole that was the vent, hearing the moronic laugh track, joining it/merging with it, thanks to the laughing gas, or whatever it is, issuing from the vent, but—and here comes a very nice ending to this debauched text—my large head, still en-noosed, is cradled in the long warm arms and bosom of my passionate early love Rhoda, known as Ro: it didn't work out with the dentist after all: he became a "professional corporation": he lacked erotic imagination: Ro, then, has come home.

TWO

Since Eros is the son of Resourcefulness and Poverty, he is fated to have the following kind of character. First of all he is continually poor and, far from being soft and beautiful as many believe, he is hard and squalid, without shoes, without a home, and without a bed.

Plato, Symposium

The AIDS epidemic is simultaneously an epidemic of a transmissable lethal disease and an epidemic of meanings and signification.

Paula A. Treichler

EROS/
Easy Rider

L.A. barrio, 1969. The Mexicans have the coke that Billy/ Captain Amerika buy then sell at a profit, become rich: the Amerikan way. Fat Tuesday for our hippies in the barrio. On the sound track: "Goddamn the Pusher Man." State-of-the-art Harleys vroom vroom: off to the Mardi Gras.

Born to be Wi-ild.

And here comes the Amerikan West, that gorgeous monster (cinematography by Laszlo Kovacs), between them and Looziana: bayou country, Carnival, local color, Cajun chow, lotsa chicks, far out.

Billy [The Kid] and Captain Amerika. Ants-in-his-pants Dennis Hopper with his Zapata mustache plays Billy, sociopath with a heart of gold. Peter Fonda: the laconic Amerika.

71

Amerika throws away his watch: "Gonna do my own thing in my own time." Who's responsible for the hokey dialogue? Fonda, Hopper, and Terry Southern. But that kind of language played: it's 1969, *after* May '68, *before* Manson '69. Icarus-winged sixties. Mucho cannabis.

Pick up a hitchhiker:
"Where you from, man?"
"It's hard to say."
"Hard to say? Where you from, man?"
"From a city."
"From a city? What city, man?"

Hopper says "man" a lot and I'll tell you why. He's a hipster, a hippie, he's the white Negro. Dig it: Billy [The Kid] Hopper did his, like, share of suffering. It was telescoped into half an hour. He says "man" a lot because he earned it.

CHRONOLOGY

1/69: Nixon: installed.
1/69: U.S. troops in Vietnam reach highest total: 544,000.
3/69: James Earl Ray pleads guilty to the assassination of Martin Luther King, Jr.
3/69: *Dionysus in 69* is performed by the Performance Group in Greenwich Village, New York. The play, derived from Euripides' *The Bacchae*, is about the "politics of ecstasy."

The hitchhiker lives in a commune in the desert, looks like Georgia O'Keeffe's New Mexico, the camera pans the inhabitants: Gosh! one beautiful/beaded/costumed hippie after another. And they're all making ritual gestures that signify "hippie." Someone's baking bread, another, barechested, is doing *Tai Chi*, others are throwing the *I Ching*: "Not every demand for change in the existing order should be heeded" (what can that mean? Be dissident but not *too* dissident? Be a good hippie?). Also: "Starting brings misfortune. Perseverance brings danger": a prevision of Hopper/Fonda's violent death. The movie is full of previsions. 1969 was full of previsions. TV sitcoms in 1969 were filled with previsions. The shelves in the suburban shopping malls in 1969 were filled with previsions.

"We have planted our seed [in this godforsaken desert], and we ask that our effort be rewarded to produce simple food for simple tastes."
"To share with our fellow man."
"In reverence to Mother earth."
"He ain't heavy, he's my brother."
Surplus value: out, surplus consciousness: in.

Back at the commune: nude swimming and dalliance in a natural spring, but no nudity in front of the camera. Hopper/Fonda and the producers will *not forfeit* their "silent majority" viewers. Meanwhile one of the commune chicks has kinda taken a shine to Captain Amerika, wants Captain Amerika to hang them up, live in sin with her in the commune. No way! Not in this cowboy movie.

Saddlin' up their Harleys. "I'm hip about time," Captain Amerika tells us in his Clint Eastwood tenor, unresonant. Peter Fonda looks like an amalgam of Henry and Jane, but without his ballast/her purchase. For some reason I remember this California guy I met in London in 1970, he was fresh from India, sick with dysentery, high from constant "transcendental meditation" which was transmitted to him in Maharishi's ashram in Rishikesh, in the foothills of the Himalayas, two or three years after the Beatles. Never mind: there will be no trashing of the hippie "lifestyle" in this text; these are the sixties "without apology."

CHRONOLOGY

3/69: Philip Roth's *Portnoy's Complaint* soars to the top of the best seller List.
3/69: U.S. secret bombing of Cambodia begins.
4/69: Armed black students relinquish student union building, Cornell University.
5/69: Jack Kerouac dies in St. Petersburg, Florida, at age forty-seven.

Fuck this heavy shit, where's Jack Nicholson at? Well, he's not at the Lakers' game in the Great Western Forum. He's not balling chicks. He's not cutting up with Warren Beatty and Harry Reems. He must be in jail. *Thas rat.* Which is where he meets Fonda/Hopper. Nicholson plays George Hanson, a wealthy wastrel lawyer with ACLU tendencies and a thick Texas accent. Decides on the spur of the moment to go to Mardi Gras with Billy and Amerika.

On the road: Nicholson: "You mean mareejuana? . . . Don't it lead to like harder stuff? . . . Yawl say it's all right? . . . All right then, how do I do it?"

Don't Bo-gart that joint, my friend. Pass it over to me.

More lyrical motorcycling through our gorgeous monster. But watch out! They's rednecks in that Eats joint just east the Tixas line, in Looziana, and they sure as shit hate niggers/ nigger-lovers/faggots/longhairs/dopers:
"You name it, I'll throw rocks at it, Sheriff."
"Hot damn!"
"I think we gone put him [Hopper] in a cage, charge admission to see 'im."
"Yankee quairs."
"I still say they won't make the parish line, Sheriff."

Well, they weren't about to get served. And they weren't about to get their butts kicked in a brawl. Besides these are your, like, Gandhian hippies not your Weathermen hippies, and so Nicholson (who in his fat cat days would play Falstaff on the stage) advised a discreet retreat.

Remember: there was this ongoing debate during the salad sixties: do you try to effect ethical changes in the world, violently, if need be? Or do you work inwardly: getting your spiritual shit together, then only after you've attained realization/wholeness/Buddhahood, do your thing in the outer world? The convenient, stoned consensus, according to a poll conducted jointly by Mobil Oil and NBC, with an error margin of plus or minus six per cent, was: Buddha-acid first, Revolution a distant second.

5/69: Police forcibly evict squatters from People's Park in Berkeley.

5/69: Brian Jones of the Rolling Stones drowns in his swimming pool in the U.K.

6/69: Stonewall Rebellion in Greenwich Village, signalling the beginning of gay activism in the U.S.

7/69: Armstrong and Aldrin walk on the moon.

7/69: *Easy Rider* premières.

7/69: Chappaquiddick.

Back on the road. Nicholson:
"You know, this used to be a hell of a good country."
Amerika: "That right? When was that?"
Nicholson has a theory: Venusians are loose among us earthlings, infusing us with their higher consciousness.
Hopper can't buy this: "How come I never heard nothin' about that?"
Nicholson: "Cause they—these Venusians—have to disguise what they're doing. They can't do it freely."
Hopper:"What the hell's wrong with freedom, man? That's what it's all about?"
Nicholson: "It's hard to be free if you're bought and sold in the marketplace."
Hopper ponders that one.
Nicholson: "You ever talk to bullfrogs in the middle of the night?"
Hopper grins: "Shit no, man. I never talked to no bullfrogs, man, in the middle of the night."

Well, the patriots pummel Nicholson to death in the middle of the night: pretty rich boy: consorted with hippie freaks/ nigger gals.
Kyrie Eleison.
Off to the fancy New Orleans whorehouse.
Billy: "He [Nicholson] would've wanted us to get laid, man."
Except Amerika ain't in the mood, Nicholson's murder depressed him, plus it reinforced his intuition of their own death. Only he's too languid not to go along.

TRACK OUT/GLOOMY DISSOLVE

Well, they've found the fancy New Orleans whorehouse and Hopper is on his fourth mint julep:

"I'm gettin' a little smashed, man. A little smashed."

Fonda: "What's happening in the streets? Like Mardi Gras?"

Turns out the guys ain't into ballin' chicks this soon after Nicholson's lynching, so they move out into the streets, Billy with his prostitute (Karen Black), Amerika with his. Carnival jollity: dancers, jugglers, grinning black folks snake dancing through the quaint streets.

In one of the best-known sequences in the film, Billy/Amerika and their chicks wend their way to the old New Orleans cemetery and you can guess what all they do there.

Drop acid, man.

Fellini-like phantasmagoria among the monuments of old AmeriKKKa. Cinematographer Kovacs pulls out the stops. And everyone has a lousy trip. And Fonda has his clearest prevision of their death.

CHRONOLOGY

8/69: Manson murders in Los Angeles.

8/69: Woodstock Music Festival in White Lake, N.Y., 500,000 participants.

9/69: Chicago 7 "Conspiracy trial."

10/69: Four violent "Days of Rage" called by Weathermen in Chicago.

11/69: Lt. Wm. Calley takes the rap for "multiple murders of civilians at My Lai, South Vietnam."

Finally they're on the road again: Billy and Captain Amerika.

"We're rich, man. We'll retire in Florida."

"You know, Billy, we blew it."

"What?"

"We blew it."

Amerika's on the money: they're blown away. Same patriots that done Nicholson. Same patriots back there in the Eats joint. From the window of their big GMC car, use a 12-gauge pump. First Billy then Amerika then the Harleys go up in flames, like institutional napalm terrorism in Nam.

Which reminds you that there have been no allusions to Vietnam anywhere in the film. Still too early in the war to take a safe position against the war and make a profit.

Anyhow: *Kyrie* etcetera for Hopper/Fonda and their state-of-the-art Harleys.

Born to be Wi-ild.

CHRONOLOGY

12/69: Police murder Chicago Black Panther leader Fred Hampton.

12/69: Hells Angels murder black man at Rolling Stones concert in Altamont, CA, the final stop in the Stones' 1969 tour.

EROS/
Skinhead

RAMBO MEETS THE AYOTOLLAH

I could feel this guy. I'm a Christian and I knew this guy was
still around. 'Cause this is my property. And so is my daughter, pink/blonde. Which is how come I'm carrying—not
AIDS, not syph, not herpes. Colt King Cobra .357 Mag is
what I'm talkin', *loaded.*

The Ayotollah is an assahollah.

Which is what they say about AIDS.

Like Sir Herbert Read said (he's from the Yookay): "All
categories of art must satisfy a simple test: they must persist as
objects of contemplation."

No problem if you're a Knight of the Realm, or a reaming
knight, there will always be an England, even if the "English"
be eating falafel on their knees facing Mecca.

Hey, suckin' Ayotollah aims to get us all on our knees, nose in each other's butt, facing Mecca. Which is how come I'm here in Honduras in camo, ass-kickin' on my mind.

Didn't say ass-*lickin'*, heck, I'm just as horny as the next Joe. OK, I'm maybe *more* horny than the next Joe, just there's a time and place for it, and like our Surgeon General said, and he's a darn good Christian himself, in spite his Ayotollah beard, I heard it's to cover an old burn scar, once a week, *maybe*, with an American-made condom and lots of soap, Ivory's best, no slick sexin', and make sure she's your wife. Face it, it's a plaguey time, thanks to Idi Amin and the Ayotollah and that other one, Libya . . .

"In suffering there is concealed a particular power that draws a person closer to Christ, a special grace. To this grace many saints owe their conversion. It could be that AIDS patients will be among our saints."

Some priest said that. They were rounding 'em up, you know, on horseback, they wore these protective blankets, I mean the horses, case the fags spit. When this priest said that about suffering and stuff.

So I papered the den in camo. My son Lance and I got it on/ got it done in one a.m. What was left over my daughter Lisa used for her locker in school. The wife would've preferred I leave it alone, the den, she loves pink, if camo came in pink no problem.

I told her it's a freakin' jungle out there. I told her if it's up to the Ayotollah our butts gonna face San Francisco and our nose Mecca, look at the interest rates.

She come back with we gotta pray. *Just Pray*, like the bumper sticker says. Well, heck, I'm not gonna say bad about prayer. Ain't nothin' stronger than good Christian prayer, 'cept, face it, ain't gonna bring the mountain to Mohammed, ain't gonna bring our purple mountains majesty to the Ayotollah. Look, only way we minister to Ayotollah is we dunk his turdy old beard in the john, which means we gone need more than prayer for the simple reason he can't understand the Christian language.

Which is how come I set up this range in the chapparal 'longside the freeway, fitted the Colt with a silencer, me and the boy. I got him a Splatmaster, air gun combat pistol, fires paint pellets, red paint, boy's darn good with it, keeps naggin' me with he wants to fire the Colt. I said Lance your hands too small, he's only ten, he wouldn't stop naggin' so I give him a chance with the Colt and he did good, holding it steady, firin' a darn good group. Ever' once in a while, firin' there in the low chapparal, next the freeway, whoosh/whoosh, I'm tempted to like turn the muzzle to the freeway, just flustration, I guess.

D.C. FATS MEETS THE BLACK SEX DEMON

Collette/

Omar Shariff/

Onassis/

Mailer/

Fleeing her rich, oppressive (and faintly revolting) sugar daddy, Traci flies to the luxurious Caribbean island of Sida Sida with little more than the dress on her back since she does not dare stop off at the condo to pack. No biggie, she outfits herself in the Sida Hilton Del Mar Boutique, and while she is trying on a strapless, cut-on-the-bias, bit of evening fluff, "Persian Ali" in his white tasseled Guccis saunters by the boutique window and catches through the side of his eye a beguiling thigh, maybe more. Ali was formerly a "Hezbollah," a fanatical Khomeini thug who beat and stoned "counter revolutionaries," but, really, politics means nothing to him. Moreover, he is massively endowed and always horny, as well as opportunistic and egomaniacal, and by introducing his active member into this or that influential circle he manages to leave mad Iran for Disneyland. However, Orange County is only fractionally less

John C.
Holmes/

Oliver
Hardy/

Gauguin/

Gidget/

Idi
Amin/

repressed than Khomeini's Persia, so Ali makes the smoggy drive to L.A. and, following his keenest instincts, becomes involved in "blue" movies, a natural lodging for his sizeable talent. However, this is around the time of the *Gospel According to Meese,* and our crusading Attorney General is in the tertiary stage of his anti-sexual-embrace campaign, which (hideous body) he confidently traces to the fainthearted "private sector" and to the diminished influence of Christian "theme parks" and to the illicit drug trade in Panama/Cuba /Colombia and ultimately to the un-moved mover in the Kremlin. With the X-rated film industry in L.A. under assault, Ali's languorous itin-erary deposits him on the fragrant /sunny/spermy isle of Sida Sida. I'll skip the small print: Traci and Ali become an item. As implied earlier, Traci is five-feet-eight and stacked, blonde of course, a sun and surf beauty from the honeyed coast of Southern California, and do you know what else? She just loves to git it on. And since her deep-sixed sugar daddy is reluctant to cancel her cred-it cards, blue-eyed Traci and her dark-skinned hunk do just like they free, white and twenty-one, right? *Not hardly.* Looming in the flies, mas-sive/ musky/merciless/ muttering in Haitian French, in his domino and death's-head mask, is the hellhound of our (post) modern Sodom:
AIDS

THE DELIRIOUS CHRONICLER MEETS
THE IMPERIAL SKINS

We see them all over southern France, clumps of shaved heads: teenage males in jeans/T-shirts/thick shoes, murdered a Tunisian bakery worker in Nice, eight "skins" stomped him while racially abusing him.

We're having an espresso, 4:30 p.m., in Toulouse, formerly "la ville rose," red structures/red politics, trade unionists, progressive students. Now the slogans on the scarred red walls are patriotic-xenophobic: *SKINS: LES VRAIS FILS DE LA NATION.*

Four sit in the next booth, thighs vibrating in spasmodic, jittery rhythm as they smoke/kick the enclosure, jerk their bodies, make laugh noises.

We'd made love as usual in the afternoon, after writing: real passion after irreal passion, or maybe the other way around. Currently reading Benjamin, writing about the old fascism, "born again" in the U.S. dominion, state of the art hate-love, fastened to the AIDS repression.

Thus sojourning in southwestern France, a different nausea, but with functional eros: Descarte's pale right hand brandishing Aquinas, his left Rabelais.

I nurse the espresso and scan *Le Monde* and pat my wife's hand and feel invaded and think of *Kristallnacht*, with the North African/homosexual enacting the Jew, and scarcely a sentence in the "progressive" press. AIDS an issue only for the far right, e.g. the Skins: AIDS-bashers, revved/noosed, "pure" Gallic blood/compressed sperm.

Scarce, though, our Skins, in Paris, polysex still packaged in Paris, unmediated sexual glances in museum galleries/bookshops/outside cinemas. In a word: Eros has here kept its purchase despite the, alongside the, hate network.

And so we have come to Byzantium, where after love I *remember* (selective in Gaul as in Silicon), eyes back in my skull, uncompelled to smile (cf. Silicon): Communes, *sans-culotte*, May '68; but also Gaul's long institutionalized hauteur, the complicity of structures, "post-structures," in the language you'd love to eat.

We're still in the Toulouse café, and if I asked the Skins to quit kicking their/our enclosure, would follow a scene out of *Cabaret*, 'tween-wars Vienna: Jew pointy-head stomped by proto-Nazis, OOM-PA/OOM-PA, Kurt Weil in counterpoint, or early Montand, before he became left then right, plus the aroma of *Schlag* and kinky sex, *interesting* sex.

At this juncture I'm tempted to summon the artist-as-shaman, an unpostmodernist conceit, I grant you, focusing with bloodshot eyes, biting one arm, with the other troweling/knifing/dripping, shaking his (her) head No, which in fact means Yes. Keeper of memories, *contre*-MEMORY, interfacing dream and real not knowing not needing to know which is which.

Me, I'll shave my head if I have to, tattoo-number my arm, force my voice, afflict the technocrat, love women's feet as in a Buñuel film.

EROS / Duras

You think you weep because
you can't love. You weep because you can't impose death.

Marguerite Duras

*You're miserable, you're loveless. You would not have done it if you
were not compelled to do it.* Would she, you wondered, go with
you, for a price?

"Go where? How much? Who are you?"

"To my cabin, actually it's a condo, in the wilderness, well,
you can hear the freeway, but only if you prick your ears. I'd
like to love you/to love, I'll pay whatever it takes."

And so you went, drove north on the smoggy freeway, in the
air-conditioned car, leased not bought (which might be an ad-
visable option for you, reader-voyeur, if so phone us at 1-800-
BUY-EROS), then west on the smoggy freeway. En route,
she:

"What kind of loving, what would you expect of me?"

84

"Utter docility. Only joking. Docility is out, and well it should be. Even geishas, with the bullish yen, did you catch this week's *Barrons?*, flip you off when you honk their Mercedes, though it isn't personal, I honk every Mercedes I see, in fellowship."

"But why me?"

"Your mouth, it reminds me of Jeanne Moreau in *Diary of a Chambermaid*, sullen but pliant, receptive to deviation, more so even than Bardot. Deneuve is another story. But you must not talk, that's a condition."

"Not talk you mean when—"

"Exactly."

"But what . . ."

But you (and she) had arrived at your destination, near the ocean, or fairly near. *Near* the ocean is choice-choice, you can only afford choice, we'll give you another year. It's a sluggish market, better make that eighteen months.

YOU: "Listen you can hear the surf. No, that's the freeway, whoosh/whoosh, day and night. It's soothing, in its way, don't you think?"

SHE: "Very nice. Your own little lovenest."

YOU: "*Lust*nest. I don't know how to love, which is why we're here together, remember?"

"You've loved women."

"I've made love to women."

"But without loving them?"

"Yes, without."

"Without being loved by them?"

"Without . . . I don't know."

SHE: "Nice champagne, dry and—what's that word they use in the Schweppes commercials, on TV?"

YOU: "Ebullient, ecumenical, eczema, enema, effervescent?"

SHE: "Scheppervescent."

YOU: "California champagne, Livermore Vineyards, up the freeway from the nuclear plant, drink as much as you like. I know the vintner, MBA from SMU, tall thin guy with bad skin out of Tulsa. He used to work in futures, grew tired of the rat race. You'd ask him a question and he'd close his eyes to think/calculate. Sold his Volvo, bought a Bronco."

"How long will you be wanting me?"

"Well that depends."

"On what?"

"On the alignment of the planets and my ego structure. To put it another way, on my ability to integrate sex and lasagne. You're smiling. Lasagne (spelled with the terminal "e"), prepared jointly in the modish kitchen, guy/gal, is to me emblematic of love, I think."

SHE: "I cook very basic. I prefer to eat out."

YOU: "Gal is wearing a brief orange vinyl apron and black high-heeled espadrilles, New Age space music on the CD, as she bustles about the modish kitchen. Congoleum tiles on the floor, or wood, white oak sanded and shined, moderate gloss. Congoleum is better. She's naked beneath her apron."

SHE: "I had a feeling."

YOU: "Except for her satiny pelt."

SHE: "What? Well, at least that's not vinyl."

YOU: "She manages to bend a lot, fetching a tupperware from a low shelf in the fridge, picking up an olive pit from the Congoleum, head down/arse up. In the process of preparing the lasagne."

SHE: "And what is he wearing, the guy?"

"Guy's wearing his red ant boxer shorts, purchased through the Lands' End catalog, upscale, out of Wisconsin, credit-card-phone-order."

"Hmm."

"Thanks to pluck, luck and opportunism, they're L.L. Bean's keenest competitor. Have some more champagne."

**

She slept on her side, one long slender arm curled behind her head, slender long back, undulant swell of buttocks (however she sat or lay, her buttocks curved/swelled). You watched her sleep, no, you felt/tried to feel her sleep, your large dry head nestled in her satiny pelt, her breathing: untroubled, creaturely.

It had been very satisfactory (as Hemingway would put it) lust, you forceful, she pliant. When in your froth you had expelled those climactic anglo saxonisms, she had, you imagined, smiled through parted lips (wide mouth, marginal overbite). "Imagined" because you were plying *behind* her (Norman Mailer). She remained, as per contract, silent, what an effort that must have been.

And then she slept, on her side, her sex, that magic, gently enclosed, sepals/petals, dewy, schweppervescent, while man-child, you, unloving, ill-loved, face pressed against the sweet-shop window/sweatshop window.

But now you pace, you step out on the terrace to hear the sea, which you hear, you think, in the brief caesuras of freeway whoosh. You slip on your Sony earphones, switch on the TV, the "Best" of Letterman, reruns through the dog days. Finally you lie down, though not to sleep. You gaze at her through most of the night: slender, taut-waisted, high-full-buttocked, soft-skinned, long legs, muscular (does that disconcert you?). A trained dancer's legs, an eloquently articulated body, frail *and* resilient, better: resilient mimicking frail because of what is still demanded of sensual woman despite the inroads of female bodybuilding and anabolic steroids. When she wakes after dawn she asks what color the sea is. You say that you do not know, but that the freeway is grey-brown, melancholy residue of Life's a Beach.

She smiles ambiguously and closes her eyes, but not before you in your morning rigor/dawning rectitude (not uncommon among vigorous menopausal males) kick off your red ant boxers, clasp her firmly: mish- mish- missionary, hoarse-throating those climactic anglo-saxonisms (she, pliant, silent, creaturely).

"Was that," she whispers, after catching her breath, "love?"

"No. I don't know. It was, I think, potent mystery/portentous misery."

And later, along the shore, which you, and your bought love, get to by crossing the freeway, the inscrutable sea, despite the oil slicks/industrial waste, and hark: a graceful girl singing as she walks. You think of Stevens' *She sang beyond the genius of the sea.* In fact she is shouting to or at herself, part of a pentecostal church outing collectively praying (though not for you), their painted-over school bus parked on the sand.

**

So the days linger, merge, pass. You sleep in her, on her, you cradle your large head against her sex, you sleep on the carpet at the foot of the waterbed. She: languorous, subdued, virtually silent, since the contractual inhibition on her voice during lust she extends to *après* lust. Except for her brief hysteria when the toilet overflows and she can't open the bathroom door to get out, and you can't reach the condo *concierge*, and neither of you knows where the turn-off valve is . . .

But that was the toilet, which is not the same as lust, despite certain reader-response analyses of Sade or Genet or Bataille or early Burroughs.

YOU: "Your body speaks, and when I am in you I *hear* you gently contracting, releasing, breathing. Out of you, like now, lying on my side on the waterbed as you sit barefoot on your billowy buttocks, your long strong legs semi-lotused on the shag rug by the fireplace, I smell your lemony fragrance but am separate from you who know love. Must I be in you to share in your knowing?"

SHE: "How many days has it been?"

YOU: "Eight. Two are left."

SHE: "And you feel how?"

YOU: "The same: pining, anarchistic, make that nihilistic, amorous."

SHE: "Have we finished the champagne?"

YOU: "Far from it, I bought two cases, you want a spritz?"

SHE: "When you are in me do you think of me?"

"I think of me being in you."

"And when you are not in me, in anyone?"

"I think of me *not* being in you, in anyone."

She gazes at you over her fluted goblet: "I wish I could pity you."

"Why?"

"Because you torment yourself, you make yourself torment yourself."

"I mean why *can't* you pity me?"

"Because you get off on it, moping/rehearsing/displaying."

"And is that why I cannot love?"

"What you love is not being able to. If I were literary I would quote Sartre on Baudelaire: 'He transformed *malaise* into a principle of conquest.' In any case you are stuck, inventorying your griefs, taunting it like a chained dog."

"Taunting *it?*"

"Taunting love. In that zesty, queer diction of yours. Come to me."

"This minute?"

"Yes. You know by now that champagne makes me randy."

You are randy, you take her, she has you take her, takes you for taking her, side by side, then yab-yum, after Shiva-Shakti, who in spite of enormous zest (Lord Shiva) destroyed love/Xeroxed love, after which you actually slept. When you woke she was gone, her imprint still on the waterbed, her pneumatic rump (ghostly), her lemony fragrance, whoosh/whoosh of the freeway. It came out to nearly two hundred fifty dollars a day for nine days.

Sipping, now, your house red at *PRINGLE'S SINGLES*, just south on I-5, you brood, recollect, envision, revise, resect, deprive, enumerate, anatomize your recent lust, tired now, depressed of course, and still amorous. Oh yes.

90

EROS/
Waldheim

Kim said: How do you know you like her?

Well, it feels right.

Kim said: She's ten years older than you.

She's nine years, well, nine-and-change years, older than me. But so what?

Kim said: It's not that she's good in bed but that she's good to *you* in bed, right? Motherly and stuff?

Motherly? I don't know. She's very tender.

Kim said: She lets you do your shit, right? One from column B, two from column A, whatever you want, she's there: her chapped thin lips opened wide for your spunk, your meager spunk.

There's a different class of panhandler now than there used to be, they just won't take no for an answer.

Kim said: And me. I'm supposed to do the sporting thing, right?, wish you luck, ducky fucking, etcetera, and so on.

So what happens if you do the sporting thing? You might actually feel better about yourself. Sporting is underrated in this country. Sporting decolonized India. Imagine if Gandhi had been dealing with the Germans. Or with the Americans, for that matter.

Kim said: You expect me to step aside like the jaded British out of India. While you'll be doing what? Colonizing your brave new Pakistan, Mama Paki, who lets you dunk your stiffened dead in her filthy Ganges any time you get the urge.

Travelers seated just two seats from her moments earlier were gone. The suction even pulled her earrings off.

Kim said: Fucking me wasn't keen enough for you. Because it turns out I'm not frail "like a woman," not insecure about menopause, about men.

You are frail, and you were keen. Fucking you was keen. It's not that.

Kim said: What did you say her name was, this sucky menopausal bitch, this plot of quicksand?

Her name is Marguerite. As in *Faust.*

Kim said: More of your self-dramatization. Who's Mephisto in this endgame of yours?

"An AIDS-inflicted mentally-handicapped 6-year-old girl *may* attend class with children her own age, but must be

kept isolated inside a glass enclosure, a federal judge ruled Monday."

Who's Mephisto? Mephisto is the IBM shareholder who walks rapidly without moving his arms.

Kim said: And what do you, Faust, figure to lose?

Mephisto is the careful smile on the face of the restroom attendant in the Harvard Club.

Kim said: What do you figure to lose?

Mephisto is the Kurt Waldheim lookalike piloting the Concorde from D.C. to U.K., the aircraft filled with our rich and famous. A *plastique* planted in a packet of condoms brought it down over Scotland. Planted, the investigators concluded, by Mau Mau Palestinian Shiites.

Kim said: I get the point: multiple-faced Mephisto. And you're Woody Allen as Noam Chomsky-Faust, the Last of the Just. What do you stand to lose?

"My husband assured me that only the strongest young man could go twice with a woman in one day? I believed him; aren't we women fools? You must have come a dozen times." "Not half that number," I replied smiling.

Everything's at stake. Everything's always at stake under Capitalism.

Kim said: I both love and hate the way your unconscious seeps into the things you say. It's something you cultivate, I know. Your ongoing agon with institutions. That hump of dreams you lug on your back. What does your new old lady think of it, Marguerite?

She seems to accept it, me.

93

Kim said: How is it different with her than with me? Physically, I mean? Does she like to be on top? Or does she let you do your horsey act? Does she pant? Does she encourage your odd propensities?

She doesn't break it down that way.

Kim said: Ha! I knew it: unreflective, unanalyzed, in collusion with your delusions: your menopausal Barbie Doll.

The sole pleasure he received was extorting from his wife the admission that she sometimes imagined the naked bodies of other men.

Kim said: Do you remember that night, after Waldheim got in, and all of Austria was toasting her native son, how crazily we made love: you, me, and . . . what's her name?

Delia.

Kim said: Right, Delia. That eighteenth-century name. Whatever happened to her? And why do I associate that richly erotic interval with Waldheim?

"And we walked down Bourbon Street and ate at Sammy's and I had a small steak and I think she had a salad and I signed the Visa card for I think it was $22 and all of a sudden the beeper went off."

Delia was a cocktail waitress, she moved to Indianapolis. As for making love crazily, it has to do with his contagious zest, Waldheim's, for life. When he served in Serbia, where those Jews and partisans were gassed, he was known as a funny, funny guy, the clown prince of the SS.

Kim said: That must be it. You put your finger on it. I remember when you'd put your fingers on, in, me. Your educated fingers. You're a swine, you know that? A user.

Really, I'm not. I have an agenda, it's true. And I like to have my id massaged. I like to think that I live life "my way," that when the opportunity arises I go for the gold. You've seen those Bud Light commercials. If all this positive thinking makes me a swine, then I stand accused.

Kim said: You've seen the *Night Porter*, haven't you? 1974?

Dirk Bogarde and . . . what's her name? British, with the sinuous neck?

Kim said: Charlotte Rampling. Do you remember that concentration camp scene with the two men—inmates—fucking? The aggressor pumping the other from behind had a delirious glint in his eyes. The passive one looked stunned but too weary to resist.

Hmm. Why do you bring that up?

Kim said: I don't know. Despair and violent sex. Waldheim and the anti-abortion forces. Our depleted ozone layer and fascist skinheads. Your cynical manipulation of your older woman.

The husband squats above the birthing wife
and about his testicles there is a
**   "noose"**
which she tugs and twists
so that he delivers his sperm
as she emits her child.

Kim said: You know something: I'm up to here with your shuck and jive. Let what's her face suck it up, your menopausal mamasan.

Kim said: You know what I resent as much as anything? You and your Casanova-ing have turned two women, two sisters against patriarchal oppression, into adversaries.

Marguerite isn't your adversary. She knows nothing about you.

Kim said: Ha!

Kim said: So what do you really want from me? A tug and a twist? A hump for the road?

Hmm. I'm hesitant to say it. But how about another interval of crazy loving? You, me, Marguerite? Because telegenic Kurt is still in. I'm talking about Waldheim. He's even had an audience with the Pope. And now with the revived interest in creamy pastries and Mozart in the wake of the dazzling success of *Amadeus* in the U.S., Austria is on a roll. I'm kidding. What do I want from you? A compassionate ear would be nice, accompanied by a few bars from the recent hit: "That's What Friends Are For," as recorded by Dionne Warwick, Gladys Knight, Stevie Wonder, and, oddly, Elton John.

"In the 40s the Nazis were big. In the 50s it was "get the commies." In the 60s the cutting edge was drugs and sex. In the 70s it was computer terrorism. In the 80s it's AIDS. Satanism is definitely the crime of the 90s."

EROS/
No Restrooms

Bunny needed to use the restroom, but she was in New York City, affectionately called Duh Terlet, while not containing public toilets, except in shops/museums/restaurants: FOR PATRONS' USE ONLY. Bunny was broke except for a subway token. True, subways contain toilets, but they are padlocked, off-limits, *verboten*, presumably because of the difficulty monitoring them. What's to monitor? Homos, the

homeless, AIDS carriers, pre-op transsexuals, Shiites, crack fiends, I could go on. Fortunately for Bunny she was near Times Square, the Great White Way, white above, black brown pitted below. Hey, what's playing in the flicks?

RAMBO'S NEPHEWS, encoring the macho-xenophobic, mega-profitable formula for the leisure lover (*leisure* being Culture Industry's *pleasure*), who happens to find herself in,

97

on, astraddle Times Square. Bunny didn't qualify, her bladder was bursting, she's only sixteen, she sings songs, moreover crabs infest those movie theaters, also predatory AIDS carriers, serious songs (whatever that means).

Speaking of high culture, Stallone himself sauntered by, disguised as a Spinal Trauma Unit administrator, wearing a blue necktie flecked with small pink wheelchairs. Bunny sighted the Port Authority Bus Terminal, where she had in fact disembarked some hours before, that cavernous box on Eighth and Ninth Avenues, near the site of the old Metropolitan Opera House, where R. Nixon

sang *Rigoletto*, the Duke's jester, humped with rancor. Bunny headed thither hoping to find a restroom, unsimulated/unmediated/vacant. Luck was with her, she entered, she squatted, golden nectar issued into the intricate cess, the macro-underbelly, where legions of dusky losers live in and around the sewers and pipings, *like vermin* (this is not well known, you won't see them if you avert your gaze),

Like the Prepuce South of the Belly of Meese.

They inhabit, I say, the infrastructure of this great city, without beepers, their very own Bangladesh. But how does she look? Give us a kiss and characterization. Bunny's lithe and blonde, dear reader/scanner, with big wide-apart blue eyes, and by golly she's built, athletic grace (the 80s demand it) and old-fashioned curves in one package. Plus she's sweet as tupelo honey (the organic kind), innocent as a just-fledged dove, a white dove, white

as the white of a stricken Ethiopian child's eye. White as the antiseptic frock worn by the millionaire oncologist making his rounds in the hospice of privilege. White as the driven snow fabricated by technology in the service of weekend skiers in temperate climates. Did

I say that Bunny actually found an employable toilet in the Port Authority Bus Terminal? Don't you believe it. The restroom on the main floor, Eighth Avenue side, was "Out of Oder" [sic]. The restroom on the Ninth Avenue side was inhabited by a bouquet of street people singing hymns to Freedom of Opportunity to the accompaniment of a jew's-harp. Bunny would have swapped a song or two for a pee, but their glares told her *Nothing Doing!* The restrooms on the "mezzanine" were inhabited alternately by Puerto Rican separatists and post-op transsexual prostitutes. Two

were Hank Kissinger lookalikes, they might have been twins, both wore beepers.

Still another restroom was accessible only to passengers to Albany and points north. Bunny, a silly millimeter away from springing a leak, was back on the street. Geez, what was she doing on the streets of the infected Big Apple, uncorseted/uncosseted, far far from the bosom of Twentynine Palms, California, just downwind of Palm Springs, a chaw's spit from Twentynine Palms Marine Corps Base? Waal, she done waved goodbye to all that, lit out for the bigs, an American tradition, don't you forget it. Goes way back to our forefathers, imperiled by bigotry, striking out for the sylvan wild across the sea, uninhabited.

Except by savages.

Her mom claims Bunny gets her notions from teevee, that much assaulted medium, though recently recuperated by semioticians and New Age Marxists, as signifying what *ain't* on America's mind. *Factoid:* she got tired of Church, the ticky-ticky of the calculator, her mom's, she's into Real Estate, works at home, never without her beeper. Tired of the desert in around above below Twentynine Palms. But, shoot, there at least she could pee, behind a Joshua tree if it came to that. Ginkgo trees *(Ginkgo biloba),* planted all over the Big Apple, the fruit foul when crushed, but they absorb the pollutants.

Bullspit! ain't nothin absorb them major league pollutants but your lungs/your bloodstream.

Competing pimps in wide hats, packin' machine pistols, spaced along Eighth Avenue from Fortieth to Thirty-third: beckon to Bunny without talking to her, whistle without whistling, stroke her not stroking. Bunny has to pee something

awful, hums a song to get her mind off it, cuts east to Seventh, something she wrote herself, sidestepping AIDS victims, eyeing blind alleys, corridors, 'bout the lack of real feeling in the world. At Thirty-First she actually tries the metal door of a four-story tenement. Locked. She keeps walking. It's August in the Apple, hot/humid/hell-bent, no sky. Did

I say that Bunny was new in town? Bussed all the way from Twentynine Palms, had her purse stolen in or around Cleveland. Is she scared? No, she's numbed. *Real*

Estate is the purr-fect career choice for housewives, especially in Twentynine Palms, which like most of the Southwest is on a roll. Which is why Bunny's mom and lots other moms are into Real Estate. Which means moms no longer instruct daughters how to insert the tampon, 'cause, one, with Church and Real Estate work and Homemaking, there's just not enough time. Two, Church

and civic leaders have rated feminine hygiene for teenage girls triple X. Gosh,

she's got to go *so* bad. Walking through Chelsea now, rundown/upscale, north of the Village. She doesn't know her way, but her instincts are sound, generations of artists before her made the trek downtown to Greenwich Village, humming on lithe legs, into the already colonized unconscious, believing in (as the American phrase has it) themselves. Since then the unconscious has been graded / paved / enchurched / infected with medical waste, except Bunny don't know it yet, shaved

lab rats, bloody syringes, human viscera. Could be she never will. Could be she's tone deaf, her small nose stuffed [with white Stetsons], selectively blind, like her kin in Twentynine

Palms. Hey, we like her just the same, and right now the big thing is finding her a pot

to pee in. She may just have to wet her drawers, dribble down her leg, her slender tanned leg, onto the grimy pocked pavement, add her fundamental signature to the hands-on cultural history of oppressed-folks-retch-on-the-city-streets: WELCOME TO PESTILENCE, LI'L SISTER (underwritten by a grant from . . .)

EROS /
Italian Love Letters

Declaration of love from a Young Man to a Young Lady:

My Dear X:

Love comes of itself and cannot be commanded.

To tell you the impression that you have produced on me would be vain, my heart has already said too much. Yet your sweet looks *(I suoi dolci sguardi)* have granted me courage to write to you.

Yes, from the day on which I first saw you, I felt myself drawn to you by an irresistible farce, which has little by little groin into a deep affliction. Now my fondest hope, said the

Manville-Executive-Art-Investor to his multi-million-dollar-Manet, is to become the companion of your lice.

Yours very devotedly,
X X

The Young Lady's Response:

Dear X X:

I do not deny that I am very much charred with your letter and if I do not fear to seem too bold, I would also say encouraged not to refute all your advances, graceful degradation, which I would fain believe *(che voglio credere)* honest and sincer.

You will however understand that I cannot honor your declaration without the consent of those on whom I am dependent and also because a young gril cannot and ought not to show her fuelings, pharmaceutical terrorism, without serious and reasonable refection.

Your obedient,
X

Demand in Marriage to the Father of a Young Lady:

Dear Sir:

Believing that concealment is not for a ma of honor *(procedere di nascosto non convenga ad un uomo d'onorre)*, and not wishing to act in a manner with which you could reproach either myself, or my family, or my association with the sound bites that make Chippendale hunks look presidential, I take the liberty of confressing to you my fond love *(fervido amore)* for your daughter X, inside whom there is a thin person just waiting to be set free.

I hope that you will reem my family and position worthy of consideration . . .

Yours respectfully,
X X

Letter from a Young Man suggesting an Assignation:

Desired One,

How huppy I should be if I could have the pleasure of passing wind a few hours with you alone without anyone to watch us, inquire into our intentions, or laugh at our endearments *(ridire quelle frasi che ci detasse amore).*

If you love me as you say, if you bong to heap i the mystemious joy of solitude the whislers of a loving hert, you will not deny me the savor of receiving kindly the proposal which I make to you.

On Sunday morning when you leave the hous, make some excuse for laving your Aunt, better stool, say you wish to visit a friend and when alone wait for me at the end of G Avenue where I shall be expricting you in fea and treblink.

Your most faithful lover,
X X

Answer from the Young Lady agreeing to the Tryst:

My dear X X,

Your suggestion (emballdened, you say, by love) has caused me such anxious thoughts that my courage has nearly failed.

My heart however which neither speaks nor refects but which, animated by passion, beats violently *(palpita violentemente)*, cannot remain long uncertain and I may tell you that so-called *Glastnost* is nothing more than Soviet-style self-promotion, I have not been able to deny your request so wormly and persuasively proffered.

Therefore I have decided to meat you on G Avenue tomorrow moaning at 9 o'cock. I have already requested of my Aunt that I should like to visit my ailig cousin Marietta . . .

Till tomorrow, then, goodbye, an lotz of kiskes in expectaration of those you say you are to give to me.

Always your
X

Letter from a Young Man requesting a private Interview:

Ravishing X,

I always thought that love, so well described by the pots, had no dangers except for the languid and sentimental, but seeing you and admiring in your many charms one of the most bountiful of Nature's woks, I am convinced of the error of my opinions.

Yes, all my prod reasomings *(tutti i miei orgogliosi ragionamenti)* have not been able to save me from an irresistible enchantment, Muso and his mistress swinging by their heels.

I seemed to love you at first sigh. A very few minutes alone would be enough to deride my fate.

Deign, them, to tell me, oh dearest X, how you receive this sincere declamation.

Batter not to writhe; paper is not a worthy medium for your most precious thoughts. The most tinder, respoctful

105

lover ought to receive them straight from your heart like a soothing balm, Libya/Nicaragua/Hiroshima/Nagasaki.

Grant me then an appointment for this evening in your gurden. A white muslin scar tied to the balcony will mean your consent.

Then at your knees *(ginocchi)*, shall speak freely of his love he who meanwhile declawes himself to be for life,

Your most devoted admirer,
X X

Letter of Severe Reproof to his Young Lady after seeing Her talking to Someone Else:

Faithless *(Perfida)* X:

How shall I reprove you? Not all the tak and wiles of which the fair sex is justly femous could exude for a moment what, alas, I saw this morning with my own eyes in this the year of the faulty condom especially the imported varieties.

I must say, it would seem that you have a very grat interest in the person with whom I saw you today in such closet conversation.

False one! where then are our vows, your fervemt promises? At last I have found you out! I loved you and would love you still but that I feel so ungry with you.

Justify yourself then or confuss your guilt *(confessa la tua colpa)*, which after a true and sincer repantence may still be in a measure excused.

Without such a justification *(Senza una tale giustificazione)* do not expect pardon from

Your miserable,
X X

Answer to the preceding Letter:

Untrusting One:

In spite of all your wraith, I am sure that you love me, you have often told me so and, daughters of Radon, also given me induspitable prooms.

On what foundation can you then doubt me, buliming that I could deceive you and lave another?

Do you know with whom you saw me in such intimate conversation yesterday mooning? It was my brother Y Y, who arrived on Tuesday from the University, where he is studying lawn.

I say no more, only in future be more cautious in firming judgements and not make a mistake which has certainly, vanilla sex lavished in religious theme parks, happened this time.

Yours forever,

X

Descriptive Letter to a Young Lady who is at a Distance:

Amorosa,

Truly if you do not hasten to return, my darling, you may find me no lager fatful to you when you do.

Yesterday evening I was at a ball, where I met a girl, Wall Street is a tender but fickle lover, almost as bellyful as yourself. She had golden hair but not like yours, a brood open forehead, but yours is still more so. Her eyebrows seemed pointed by Raphael! *(I suoi sopraccigli sembrano dipinti da Raffaello!)*

Her eyes which were a deep block while yours are blue, had in every glands a new conquest. They had as much vivacity as yours have swetness *(quanta dolcezza hanno i tuoi)* and seemed made to command love, as yours are made to inspore it.

Her cheeks were of a delicate ruse which seemed a wok of tart, while instead it is a gift of nature who has showered on her so many grifts that excerpt for yourself (who are her masterpiece) *(chesei il suo gran capolavoro)*, she would be the finest of her works.

Her mouth, while not tinny like yours, is smaller than any I have ever admired. Her lips are so trash and rosy that you never in all your life saw anything more lovely, and as for her teeth *(quanto ai denti)*, they are so white and reglar, with two red, white and blue saber-like fangs surgically implanted in each jaw, that you feel inclined to tell all sorts of gay stories to make her laugh so as to have a chance of seeing them benter.

You can well imagine how difficult it was for me to reman indifferent before, AIDS-victim as terrorist, such a divine creature.

If ever you thank of deceiving me, beloved X, take care at least that the person that you prefer *(la persona che me preferiraia)* have as many fine qualitities as she of whom I write whose faskinations I have rezested.

Think: today is the twentieth day since I sawd you, an eternity, I can no longer beer the bain of your assence. Pining, I am

Yours,
X X

Sending a Lock of Hair to a Lover:

Dear Heart,

You have asked me several times for a lock of my hair *(ciocca de' miei capelli)* to put in a gold locket and keep in memory of me who have, Mobil Presents Moravia, loved you for so loog.

It is not the smellness of the gift that you should think of but the greatness of the sacrifice I make in sending you that which is nearer the hert of a woman than anything else save the ideological "mores" that impel the doting female to mutilate her body.

Your most devoted,

X

Rejoicing at having obtained a rich Dowry:

My Adored X,

I know that your gool uncle Antonio has given you a considerable sum as dowry so that at our appoaching marriage your financial worth may be increased.

This makes you huppy and thus I also rejoie because greed, not fear, is the driving force in this market, said Andrew Lebow, an oil analyst with Shearson Lehman Brothers.

As you well know, I love those that lavish you, and I am most happy that soon I shall be able to say: "You are mine," feminist ideology, whether progressive or bourgeois, rejects male patronage.

Your doting,

X X

Letter from a Young Man far from his Lady writing to tell Her that he has dreamt of Her:

My Hope,

It seems impassible that a lover's fency should try to console itself even during the hours of sleep. Yet last night I was sheated and hold in my arms my bellyful girl, who looked at me tinderly while I never tired of gaziny at hr. From time to time we opened our mouts to zay a few words: "Do you lave me?" "Yes dearly." And our lips then muet, and shall I tell you? Met in a kiss so tendo that we were in the seventh heaven *(un 'estasi di paradiso)*. Then you threw up your arms round my nek embracing me, but as I put my art round you to drawl you towards me I awoke. I feel thankful for sech a delightful dram.

Cuntinu then to lave me as in the pist and believe in the legacy of Rockefeller who slaughtered rights activists in Attica, with eternal love and many sighs as I kuss you,I swear I am, Rocky dead in the arms of Venus, a corporate gal with spectacles, but pliant.

Forever,
X X

Laconic Dismissal to a Sweetheart:

I know all! It is enough! *(Mi basta!)*
Goodbye Meese.
Hallo Kirkpatrick.
Cum all over me face Occidental Petroleum.

EROS / Amsterdam

RED LIGHTS

-Please. How does one operate this dispenser?
-Put your guilder in, pull the bloody lever, your condom will pop right out.

**

-You speak English?
-Little.
-I'm looking for a Chinese supermarket.
-What?
-Chinese supermarket. I understand there is one very close to here.

- Supermarket?
-Right. Where they sell Chinese goods. You know.
[Pause]
-I think you want to go there, Zeedijk.
-Where?
-Pointing: Zeedijk.
-Zeedijk. Thank you.

**

When the red light is on but the opaque curtains drawn, the woman is entertaining, the consensus price is fifty guilders for "fucking/sucking," more eccentric sex available at selected stations at higher rates.

**

-Do you speak English?
-I do.
-I'm representing someone who is interested in purchasing videos with young boys.
-No.
-You don't have any?
-No.

**

Bloedstraat. The women in the windows up and down this street are Indonesian. The Sikh tourist taps him on the shoulder, asks whether he knows how to operate the dispenser.
The mallards shriek in the canal.
-Put your guilder in, pull the lever, your condom pops right out.

**

-Do you speak English?
-Okay.
-I'm representing someone who is interested in purchasing videos or magazines with young boys.
-You are representing?

112

-That's right.

**

The narrow eighteenth-century structure on OZ Voorburgwal opposite the canal is a sex shop. He ducks his head to enter.
-I understand there is a Chinese supermarket very close to here, speaking slowly, distinctly.
-What?
-Chinese supermarket? Where they sell Chinese goods?
The young black man (probably Surinamese: old Holland's far-flung empire) scratches his head. The difference between this sex shop and American over-the-counter varieties? Golden showers, unsimulated S & M, routine anality.
-I think you want to go there, just north, the Zeedijk.
Outside he consults his Baedecker. Turns out Camus' *La Chute* was set in this same run-down street, Zeedijk, in a bar called Mexico City (actually called Berlin). It's still there, he goes inside, sits at the bar, orders *oude* Genever. Just past two in the afternoon, Monday, raining. Two other men, smoking, nurse their drinks at the other end of the bar. Genever is subtler than gin, easier going down.
He walks the length of Zeedijk, for a time walking behind a man, drunk or drugged, who is brutalizing his dog, a Belgian Shepherd cowering with its tail between its legs. The man screams at the dog while jerking crazily at the short chain around its neck.
He crosses the narrow street, emerges at Warmoesstraat: no Chinese supermarket.

**

After dark the prostitutes switch on their special lamp: become luminous behind their windows, frozen into a pose that displays their best feature. Or they dance or stretch languidly. Tend to be ghettoized according to race-nationality: Dutch, African/Surinamese, Moroccan, Spanish, Asian.

**

-Please, you tell me how to do this?
-Stick your guilder in the slot, pull the lever and your condom pops right out. But save your money, friend, the women all supply condoms.
-They supply?
-Right. With their services.
Could be the Sikh tourist has something else in mind: he inserts his guilder, pulls the lever, pockets his condom.

**

If this were '68, he would detail his encounter with the woman in the window at OZ Achterburgwal, near Spooksteeg. But readers/scanners of the 80s are leery of sexual candor, of lust unleavened by love & marriage. Well, it was rapid more than tender, she had access to an alarm to contact the police should the client prove unruly; he resisted deviation.

**

The bourgeois like to keep their curtains open, their tidy households on display: well-tended plants and books and wall-coverings and cushioned easy chairs and antimacassars and TV. The Dutch call it *gazellig*, cozy: the passerby is welcome to look but not to stare. This display extends to the prostitute, quasi-naked/luminous in her tidy brothel room with its brocaded bed and spotless bidet and stuffed animals and knick-nacks. The passerby is encouraged to look and either to enter or pass by. Please, no extended scrutiny.

A young man lives across a narrow courtyard from a middle-aged widower whom he sees daily at his meals; in his tidy, cozy sitting room; etc. When occasionally the young man goes to the widower's bicycle shop they enact business without acknowledging that they know each other.

The "intimacy" across the narrow courtyard is impersonal, ritualized, segregated. So too, the naked, luminous girls in the windows will sell their bodies with courtesy/without intimacy.

114

**

-You speak English?
-Yes.
-I'm representing someone who is interested in buying videos or magazines with young boys.
[Pause]
-How young?

**

-Would you happen to know of a Chinese supermarket in this area?
He has collared a policeman, oddly scarce in the Red Light district.
Inclining his head: -What you ask?
-Chinese supermarket?
-Ah. Well. Yes. You know Zeedijk?
He returned to Zeedijk. The man mistreating his dog was gone, but the narrow gutters were filled with men who'd mistreat their dogs, or anyone's dogs. He's given hard looks, but it's too early in the day to get mugged.
Surprise: he found his "China Super Market," a narrow basement sex shop neatly crammed with magazines, videos, "sex-aids," all with an Asian accent.

LETTER TO A WOUND

She was, he decided, Moroccan: sinuous, languorous, olive-skinned, barefoot. Nearly all the other prostitutes wore high-heeled shoes or slippers with their skimpy costumes. Her feet were slender and high-arched, their bottoms soiled.
Her window was directly across the narrow *steeg* from another Moroccan, shorter, plump, with a guileless smile, wearing mules. The two girls (they couldn't be older than eighteen) were friendly: gesticulating, laughing with each other via the windows, too cold to go outside.
That drizzly Monday was the first time he saw her, the Red Light district thin of tourists, office workers on their lunch

break, mallards and coots contented/contentious in the canal with the rain and lunch remnants. In her fire-engine red halter top and matching G-string, she lay back in the chaise longue, long legs/pointed feet, a wide adolescent smile on her face. When he passed she caught his eye. He walked around the block, passed her again and her eyes gestured to him.

What was in her eyes? A ritualized come-hither, but more than ritual, less game than play, the not-yet denatured play of a teenaged Moroccan: gorgeous and poor and the wrong gender / color.

On Damrak, just west of The Lights, was an American Express office where he changed dollars for guilders. Raining harder. He waited for a number 4 tram, settled on a 25, which dropped him near Berlage Bruge, five minutes east of his flat on Amstelkade.

The following day, Tuesday, taken up with engagements: a herring lunch in the Jordaan, the "Torture Instruments Through the Ages" exhibit on Heiligeweg, a lager in a "brown bar" on Spui.

Wednesday he wrote, that is, typed on his old Olivetti, facing the canal (grey heron, black-headed gull, great tit, *Parus major*). What was he writing? Words and music about physical love in the time of AIDS. What's AIDS? A highly infectious disease generated by God/spread by ideology.

The single concession to AIDS in The Lights could be found on the individual windows. Along with notices like *No Photos, Please; For Rent, Phone;* there was: *Be Safe, Enjoy, Use Condoms,* in Dutch/English/German/French/Japanese.

Wednesday p.m., unseasonably mild: he caught the tram at van Woustraat, punched his ticket, found a seat, loosened his scarf, exchanged smiles with a thirtyish woman with the high forehead and pink translucency of a Vermeer.

Tonight the Red Light district was full of locals, junkies, junkets (male and female Japanese, their state-of-the-art Toyota tour bus safely stowed on Damrak), lust-fantasying males of various persuasion. But she was depressed.

Luminous under the special light, she was stretched out on her chaise in a thigh-length black lace camisole and black G-string, barefoot. He walked slowly past then turned the corner and walked past again. She gazed at him not seeing him, her large black eyes without light.

He watched as a man, a Sikh tourist, turbaned, bearded, fussy-seeming in his suit/tie/topcoat, paused, walked past, backed up, moved forward, backed up, finally went in. She got up, scarcely raising her eyes, closed the curtains.

He paused for an espresso on Oudekerksplein, returned to her window twenty minutes later, the curtains were open, she was on her chaise as before, luminescent and flat as a representation of a courtesan in an illuminated manuscript.

He returned one more time an hour or so later on his way to the tram and her curtains were closed. He was tempted to hang around, see who was in there with her, in fact he lurked about for a time: whoever it was, was having a long session, he grew tired of waiting and headed for the tram.

Thinks the reader: why the coyness? Why doesn't he suck in his gut and have a go? Or if it's moralizing on his mind, why not give her some guilders and pack it in? Stop skulking.

What can I tell you? He's a skulker, skulking is what he does. Is yours (gentle reader-scanner) a heart large enough to admit a skulker?

He even skulks when he sleeps, dreaming about this and that, slipsliding from one lure to another, foraging kindling (as it were) for another round of flame and farce at the clink-clink Olivetti.

Which is where you'll find him on the following gray morning: tousle-haired in wide-wale cords, Ragg wool socks, clogs, foul-weather sweater, strong coffee in his mug, no pipe: canonical image of our middle-aged writer in atmospheric exile.

But what was it about her, the Moroccan girl, that set her apart from the hundred-odd others in The Lights?

Her bare feet, as he noted, pointed/high-arched. Her Semitic center. Her connection (in his head) with half-Algerian Camus' *Chute.* Her black dreaming eyes. Her deterritorialization. Her softness, she was soft, she reminded him of . . . him.

Friday evening she was up, dancing, that is moving her body rhythmically/manically, while standing, not moving her legs, grinning, her eyes charged, sighting him as he passed, not seeing him. He knew, he thought, why. The night before he'd watched as two North African men entered her space with a kind of sullen authority, the curtains stayed open. Listless, she followed them to the rear then down stairs he hadn't

117

noticed before. Seven minutes later they were back up, the men sullenly left.

And tonight, Friday, she burned with a corrosive cold flame. Tonight he had to get closer, if not yet close. He poked his head in, she grinned at him without recognition, her body in motion, her space sweetly (too-sweetly?) fragrant. He asked what her rates were, she responded in French, matter-of-factly, the voice soft, contralto, oddly self-contained.

He thanked her and left.

Where did he go? He circuited the area from Grimburg Wal to Zeedijk. Nearly all the live show porn venues were called Rossi (Mafia?). Who's hissing? Look at that! a fury of swans, mute swans (*Cygnus olor*), three of them, bills pointed down, wings arched, hissing/gliding among the mallards and debris, in the canal near Stoofsteeg.

In the upper floors of the narrow canal houses he saw people and book shelves in a mild light that reminded him of old New York where he grew up half in, half out of imaginings. He thought of Walter Benjamin in Marseilles (hashish/head-lust/hermeneutics/Nazis). As if on cue, half-a-dozen Dutch skinheads bristled by en route to brutality. The first skins he'd seen in A'Dam.

Stopped at a basement bar for a Genever. The men on either side of him were rolling cigarettes. Though a nonsmoker, he felt like smoking, stick something in his mouth (that something was *she*, the/his Moroccan).

He returned to her window but she wasn't there. Her red light was out, her curtain drawn. Curious. Why would she leave on a Friday evening at eight-forty? And so suddenly? He'd talked with her less than an hour ago.

He was tempted to ask someone, the Moroccan girl in the window opposite, but her curtains were drawn with the red light on: engaged.

He lingered/skulked. He walked to Nes, just east of Rokin, had dinner at a student "mensa": falafel, brown rice, cucumber salad, herb tea. He read about renewed terrorism in the friendly skies in *USA Today*, the "international" edition. A frequent flyer quoted as saying: "When I was detained and grilled for two hours by El Al, it was intimidating and humiliating and I never felt so confident and reassured."

After falafel he walked to Nieuwmarkt where he caught the metro. The following morning he read instead of wrote: a Nicolas Freeling sleuth deal set in the Dutch provinces. As usual, Freeling was brilliant and lateral: rumination/lucubration but where's the suckin' pathos? *He and insolent scribblers like him should be lined up against the retaining wall of an imperial city—Afrikaans, say—and executed with a Gatling gun.*

Wasn't Freeling's fault, our man in Amsterdam was restless and, frankly, worried. He mailed some letters, bought fruit and bread and good Dutch beer and mineral water. He sat on a bench near the river and watched the ducks/coots/gulls and underrated, irrepressible magpies *(Pica pica).*

Finally, two p.m., about when things get started in The Lights. He caught a 4 northbound to Damrak where he stopped at the American Express office to change dollars into guilders. A discouraging business with the dollar stubbornly in decline, despite the earnest assurances of Donald Trump and Malcolm Forbes.

Hang on! It was Saturday, what was American Express doing open? For the answer to that and kindred conundrums, read my *Inspector Libido and the Case of the American Express Office That Refused to Close.*

The wind had picked up, he put on his Irish tweed cap which he carried in his shoulder bag, not just wind but drizzle, or sleety rain, filthy stuff. He pulled his cap down/scarf up, pushed his way across the wide street, past the Grand Hotel Krasnapolsky, walked north along the canal (mallards squawking cheerily) and *she wasn't there,* but neither was the girl across from her, it was still early, and with this weather! Nonetheless other lights *were* on, and no dearth of consumers, huddling/gawking.

Walked to Nieuwmarkt where he bought a copy of the London *Times* and stopped for a coffee and read about the royal family: the melancholic Prince was marking his fortieth. His mind moved from Charles to Hamlet to . . . himself, though only fleetingly, without scrutiny, which would compromise his compulsions, which he needed, as you must know, to elude the mind police.

When he got back to her window it was four-thirty, she was still not there, though her friend was, languid/smiling. He

119

hesitated then poked his head in her door. In French, halting-ly, he said he was waiting for her friend, and would she be back by tonight.

-*Bien sûr*, she smiled.

He nodded, left, then wished he'd asked what *time* tonight? He walked west past Central Station, then south to the Athe-naeum Boekhandel on Spui, where he browsed about the in-ternational books and newspapers. Then walked to the large flower market mounted on houseboats on the Singel canal. The rain had stopped, it had warmed somewhat, lots of cou-ples out looking very sixties in their long hair and anything-goes garb and soulful expressions.

It was contagious, he felt himself feeling sixties: sensual/sentimental/apocalyptic/Buddhist: what a lovely time that was. Five-twenty p.m., still too early for dinner. He walked west then north to the Anne Frank House; coincidentally, he saw his second clutch of skinheads, four, on the other side of Prinsengracht, bristling/revving/careering.

Still inhabited by nostalgia, he walked into the Jordaan imagining Dublin, old London, older New York: that mild light where dream intersects with the everyday and *glazes* it. He stopped at an Indian/Surinamese restaurant and ate lei-surely while reading *USA Today*, only laying the paper on the table upside down. All the items in *USA Today* are brief, as you know, most are captioned, user-friendly, even upside down, don't just take my advice, try it.

He got back to The Lights at 8:40, and the area was hop-ping. He turned her corner somewhat nervously, with reason: she was still not there. Her curtains were now open, her chaise in its accustomed place behind the window, the knick-nacks (porcelain toy poodle, cuddly koala, ornamental hoo-kah, etc.) still on the windowsill, but the light was off, the sweet space void.

Her friend was of course there, and busy, light on/curtains drawn.

What now?

He walked rapidly west, then south to the "Cinecenter" on Rembrandtsplein, caught the 9:20 showing of *D.O.A.*, a re-make of the forties thriller featuring Edmond O'Brien as the poisoned accountant, the slow-acting poison killing him as he frantically tracks down his killer. In the remake, the accountant has become a lit prof who is also a failed novelist. The car chases and gun fights that monopolize the second half of the movie take place in and around a "typical" American university where the coeds all look like Gidget.

When he got back to The Lights it was nearly midnight and she still wasn't there. Again he poked his head in her friend's door and enquired, would she—the other—be back tomorrow?

This time she shrugged her shoulders, and she wasn't smiling, she looked—young as she was—beat, her eyes puffy.

He nodded, backed off.

The trams and metro quit running at midnight, so he walked back to his flat, it took him an hour and twenty minutes, dismally ruminating all the way.

It wasn't easy, but he kept himself from going to The Lights for two days and nights, returning there on Tuesday, a few minutes past eight.

She's back! Sepals, petals: he enters the sweet space. Silk, she. Sandalwood, he. Her body moves in circles, and the circles glide, collide, softly. He's not sandalwood but date palm, erect/fruitful in the Sufi sky in the remote oasis. While she, acrobatic, sips, trills, twists on his boughs, shoots, trunk . . . Green and gold and moist: Morocco.

The preceding passage is a kind of poetry, or enriched prose. It's a lie. Not only was she *not* there, another girl, also North African, was in her space and on her chaise, with the same knicknacks on the windowsill. She was slim, about eighteen, in a satiny turquoise chemise and matching G-string, and wearing ivory velvet slippers.

It was, he knew, bad form to stare, but she didn't seem to mind, in fact smiled back at him: a ritualized come-hither smile, granted, yet more than ritual, less game than play, the not yet denatured play of a teenaged North African: gorgeous, poor, and the wrong color/gender.

NOTES

The quotation from Buckley in the epigraph to Part One originally appeared on the Op-Ed page in the *New York Times* on March 18, 1986. But I found the quotation in Simon Watney's *Policing Desires: Pornography, AIDS and the Media* (University of Minnesota Press, 1987).

The quotation from Paula A. Treichler in the epigraph to Part Two is from her "AIDS, Homophobia, and Biomedical Discourse: An Epidemic of Signification," in *AIDS: Cultural Analysis, Cultural Activism*, ed. Douglas Crimp (MIT Press, 1988).

The "Chronology" in "Eros / Easy Rider" has been culled from several sources, including: *1968*, ed. Ronald Fraser (Pantheon, 1988); and *The Sixties Without Apology*, ed. Sohnya Sayres, et al. (University of Minnesota Press, 1984).

"Eros / Talk Dirty" is a pastiche-deconstruction of an article called "Talking Dirty" by Lucy Loveless in *CITYWEEK* [a Manhattan weekly], August 1, 1988.

CITY LIGHTS PUBLICATIONS

Angulo de, Jaime. INDIANS IN OVERALLS
Angulo de,G & J. de Angulo. JAIME IN TAOS
Artaud, Antonin. ARTAUD ANTHOLOGY
Bataille, Georges. EROTISM: Death and Sensuality
Bataille, Georges. STORY OF THE EYE
Bataille, Georges. THE TEARS OF EROS
Baudelaire, Charles. TWENTY PROSE POEMS
Baudelaire, Charles. INTIMATE JOURNALS
Bowles, Paul. A HUNDRED CAMELS IN THE COURTYARD
Brecht, Stefan. POEMS
Bukowski, Charles. THE MOST BEAUTIFUL WOMAN IN TOWN
Bukowski, Charles. NOTES OF A DIRTY OLD MAN
Bukowski, Charles. TALES OF ORDINARY MADNESS
Burroughs, William S. THE BURROUGHS FILE
Burroughs, William S. THE YAGE LETTERS
Cardenal, Ernesto. FROM NICARAGUA WITH LOVE
Cassady, Neal. THE FIRST THIRD
Choukri, Mohamed. FOR BREAD ALONE
CITY LIGHTS REVIEW #1: Politics and Poetry issue
CITY LIGHTS REVIEW #2: Forum AIDS & the Arts issue
CITY LIGHTS REVIEW #3: Media and Propaganda issue
CITY LIGHTS REVIEW #4: Literature / Politics / Ecology
Cocteau, Jean. THE WHITE BOOK (LE LIVRE BLANC)
Codrescu, Andrei, ed. EXQUISITE CORPSE READER
Cornford, Adam. ANIMATIONS
Corso, Gregory. GASOLINE
David-Neel, Alexandra. SECRET ORAL TEACHINGS IN
    TIBETAN BUDDHIST SECTS
Deleuze, Gilles. SPINOZA: PRACTICAL PHILOSOPHY
Dick, Leslie. WITHOUT FALLING
di Prima, Diane. PIECES OF A SONG: Selected Poems
H.D. (Hilda Doolittle). NOTES ON THOUGHT & VISION
Ducornet, Rikki. ENTERING FIRE
Duras, Marguerite. DURAS BY DURAS
Eidus, Janice. VITO LOVES GERALDINE
Eberhardt, Isabelle. THE OBLIVION SEEKERS